ACE CARROWAY
AROUND THE WORLD

GUY WORTHEY

ACE CARROWAY AROUND THE WORLD

This is a work of fiction. Names, characters, places, and incidents are either the product of the author's imagination or are used fictitiously. Any resemblance to actual persons, living or dead, is entirely coincidental.

Cover design: Ioana Ramona Cecalasan

ISBN: 198618904X
ISBN-13: 978-1986189040

Printed by CreateSpace

Westing Press

To the memory of my dad.

They shall grow not old, as we that are left grow old:
Age shall not weary them, nor the years condemn.
At the going down of the sun and in the morning,
We will remember them.

— Laurence Binyon

VOL. XCI—NO. 115

Boston Evening Globe

Evening **1C** Edition
Closing Market Prices

BOSTON, TUESDAY EVENING, MAY 24, 1921—FOURTEEN PAGES

PRICE ONE CENT

▲ ▲ ▲ EVENING EDITION—7:30 LATEST ▲ ▲ ▲

Mayor dedicates new opera hall. The Hon. Chesswick Fletch cut the ribbon at noon, but the champagne flowed well into the night, according to society sources. The new 2000 seat hall has no private boxes, though it does have plentiful balconies to offer rarefied air to the upper crust. Seats on the floor can be afforded by ordinary citizens. promises T. Oswald Boone. program director. The first opera will be none other than La Traviata, he says. The popular opera opens next month for a run of eight performances. The opera is demanding on the soprano lead, whom Boone hinted might be Edith

Clipper ship auctioned. The tall ship Coralee was purchased at public auction today by Mr. Marcus Dyer of Shreveport. He plans to returbish the storied vessel, which reportedly rounded Cape Hope thirty times. "She'll sail again," the gentleman promised, "but she won't founder in a calm. She'll be fitted with an oil burner and a screw."

Temperance meeting heated. A contingent of hecklers disrupted a meeting of the Trent Auxiliary Temperance Society last night. The invasion of loud and boisterous individuals took place at about 7:30 in the

The clipper ship Coralee at anchor. The Coralee was purchased yesterday by Mr. Marcus Dyer of Shreveport.

Pilot to fly solo around the world. Cecilia "Ace" Carroway is at it again. Not content with breaking the powered flight altitude record last fall, the famed flyer told the Evening Globe that she plans a circumnavigation of the world. Weather will control the timing of the ten-stage journey, the pilot explained. Ace Carroway is known for her wartime capture of an X8 dirigible and later aerial exploits as a civilian, including speed and altitude records. the latest one of which was set with a single-engine Lockheed Flyer, heavily customized by Carroway in order to improve speed

Chapter 1

Ace Carroway strode into the house. She stripped off her flyer's cap and goggles and wedged them partly under her wide belt. "Dad?" she called. "I'm home!"

A piece of paper sat on the divider. She picked it up. It was a letter from her father, Grant Carroway, the self-made shipbuilder and shipping magnate. The name "Darko Dor" leapt off the page, causing a nauseous twisting sensation in Ace's gut.

My dearest daughter,

Apologies, but I may be late for supper. A gentleman that wishes to sign a contract also needs to catch an outbound ship. Out of the kindness of my heart, I agreed to see Mr. Darko Dor before he departs for Istanbul.

I am eager to see you and I wish to hear what you learned in Nepal. I'll only be an hour late, at most.

Yours always,
Dad

"I sure don't want to tell him what happened in Nepal," Ace muttered. "But, Darko Dor? Gads. It's not a common name! Could it really be he? I assumed he was dead!"

A furrow appeared between her eyebrows. She drummed her fingers on the divider.

"If it's Darko Dor, what does it mean? It would mean I didn't kill him, for one! Even if it is him, it could be a coincidence, and he just wants something shipped overseas. But what if it's not? He doesn't know Dad, but he sure knows me."

Ace's gold irises contracted. "Revenge? Dad could be in danger! Where would Dad go for a contract signing? The port office?" She stuffed the letter into the shoulder pocket of her plain civilian flight suit.

She stalked to the wall telephone and dialed "0." She waited impatiently. Finally, the earpiece crackled to life.

"Operator."

"Operator, connect me with the Carroway Shipping business office, Hyannis, Cape Cod."

"Right away, ma'am."

There was a pause.

The pause stretched.

The operator said, "I'm sorry, there is no answer."

Ace's eyes narrowed. It was a few minutes after five o'clock. Someone should still be there, if only to lock doors and turn out lights. Ace hung up the mouthpiece and sprinted for her roadster, parked outside.

Homicides always happen at mealtimes. At least for me. The Carroway case sure followed the rule. It was quitting time for people that aren't police lieutenants. My belly growled for one of those French dip sandwiches from Ross's Sharkbite, or maybe a bowl of chowder. But I wasn't going to get a dip, French or otherwise. What I got was the dispatcher yelling at me.

Mind you, Marge yells at me all the time, but this time it wasn't about my clothes or mustard stains or being slobby with coffee or uncouth with donuts.

"Shots heard at Carroway Shipping, Lucy!" Marge yelled.

Lucy, well, that would be me. Lieutenant Drew Lucy, Hyannis, Cape Cod Police Department. P.D., for short.

I put my hat on. I grabbed my overcoat. It was five o'clock on the dot.

I hurried, but not too much. The boys on patrol would beat me there. We had a fancy radio dispatching system in Hyannis. Marge only yells at me after she yells into the radio microphone.

I left my gun. Had I left it in the desk? Hanging on my chair? It wouldn't matter. All the boys had guns.

Plus, this is Cape Cod, not New York.

I didn't tell Marge good night on my way out. That would have been counterproductive. If she ever found out I wasn't a purebred ogre complete with pedigree I would be doomed to make small talk with her. That's a fate too hideous to contemplate.

The weather was unsettled, almost stormy. If a proper Nor'easter had a kid brother, that's what this night was like. A few spits of rain. Gusts of wind that sounded fierce but when they blew past they barely pushed.

I took my rattletrap Model T over to Carroway

Shipping. It had the electric window wiper that came out a few years back, and I made use of it in the rain. A minute before I arrived at the shipping office, an ambulance whizzed by me, sirens blaring, heading away from where I was heading to.

The shipping office nestled next to the port, but uphill and private. Trimmed bushes lined the paved driveway. The driveway fanned out into a parking area. All the boys were at the shipping company, every patrol car we had in the Hyannis P.D. All three of them. The boys were jumpy, too. They pounced on me before I was halfway out of my car.

"Two bodies, Lieutenant! And the secretary just got carted off to the hospital. He was unconscious. Shot at least twice."

"Thanks, Bob. I see the blood." It spread in a sizeable Rorschach blot all over the pavement, its gloss kept fresh by the rain spritz.

"I'm Bill. Bob's over there."

"Whatever."

Faintly, I could hear the sound of a phone ringing from inside the office as I scouted the ground. "If the medics were here tromping around, I'll just scratch footprints off my things to watch for." I was grouchy.

"The bodies are inside the office, Lieutenant."

"Is anybody going to get the phone?"

The boys looked at each other in disarray. I snorted and walked briskly to the office. They fell in behind me. The Carroway Shipping office was a compact rectangle. The parking lot butted against the front door. The front door led to reception. Behind reception, three office doors sat in a row. A phone on the reception desk jangled, but it stopped ringing before my hand touched it. I examined the orderly desk. Nothing stuck out as unusual. I turned around.

All the boys were behind me, clustered like owl babies or something, following their mom with big eyes. They were all pretty green. The Hyannis P.D. saw a lot of retirements just after the Great War. I transferred in from Chicago, happy enough to take the pay hike and promotion. The boys thought I was used to busting gangsters every day. I let them assume. I don't talk about all that. It's in the past.

I told the boys, "No blood, here. So the secretary wasn't shot until he was outside."

Bill, or maybe Bob, replied, "That's what we figure, Lieutenant. He was all laid out, bullet holes in his back. I think he was running away from … this." The uniformed Blue gestured to the main back office. The door had a classy nameplate with dignified teeny weeny lettering, "Grant Carroway." The door stood ajar.

"Don't crowd me," I said. "And one of you ring up the operator and see who called a second ago."

I made my way into the owner's office and winced. The room had a view in two directions, a nice panorama of Port Hyannis, but three bullet holes punctured the glass. Fresh, I assumed. I thought I could see a couple or three bullet holes in the walls. I'd check for sure in due time.

Body number one was right by the door. Male, black hair, Caucasian, brown eyes, heavy brows, and a birthmark over his left eye. He wore street clothes, almost new. A couple of bullet holes in his chest made grisly stains. The strangest items were the leg braces. Metal cages clasped above and below both knees, hinged together with a fake knee joint. I spotted two canes. This fellow could hobble, maybe hustle, but not run. A gun lay beside him. A German Luger, Great War vintage. I bent and flipped his coat open. Two shoulder holsters. One full of gun, one empty.

I stepped over body number one. The flock clustered in the doorway didn't follow. I half expected to hear chicken clucks.

I padded around the big, fancy desk. Flecks of blood spoiled the nice polish. Its drawer was open. Several more canes leaned in a stand in the corner. An executive-style chair lay tipped over. The victim sprawled by the chair. Male, graying brown hair neatly cut, Caucasian, couldn't see his eyes, tailored suit, shiny shoes. He looked positively presidential, except for the bullet holes. Lots of bullet holes. His finger was still stuck through the trigger guard of a Smith & Wesson snubnose. Just the sort of gun an executive would stash in his desk drawer.

Two chairs for visitors sat in front of the desk. Grant Carroway had enjoyed his own private telephone. A short stack of sheets of paper on the desk faced so that a visitor could read them, but askew. A contract, perhaps. Other things, fountain pens, index cards, file cabinets, ledger books; they all blended in.

I tried to ignore my rumbling gut. Why always mealtimes?

CHAPTER 2

All of a sudden, the hairs on the back of my neck prickled. I turned toward the doorway and the cluster of blue uniforms. They had parted like the Red Sea for Moses. But it wasn't Moses, not even close. It was a dame. The gawking chicken posse noticed that point right off. They forgot the dead bodies awfully quick, that's for sure.

The dame was all wrong. Too tall, dressed in coveralls and not a proper skirt, darker skin like a Jamaican or something, and a face full of bad attitude that I was about to collide with like shoe leather and sidewalk.

I spluttered in exasperation to the boys, "Keep journalists out of the crime scene, please, officers!" I pasted on a fake smile. "Ma'am, this is a police investigation. Members of the public are not—"

She cut me off like *she* was in charge. My jaw clenched. She got under my skin faster than rattlesnake fangs.

"I am Cecilia Carroway. Where is my father?"

The boys reached for her elbows, but hearing her name made 'em go limp. It deflated me a little, too. I minced back toward the door, stepping over body number one. I held up my hands, palms out. "You don't want to see, ma'am. I'm sorry. I'm not even sure it's him, but if it is, your father's dead."

I hated saying that. It made it personal. Bodies and

blood become part of the job. But seeing the shock set in on her face is something I will always remember, and something I will always want to forget.

Her gold-colored skin blanched and she weaved on her feet like she was suffering vertigo. No hysterics, though. No tears. She said, numbly, "Curse you, Darko Dor!"

I blinked. She knew things, apparently. I reached for my notebook and pencil stub. "Who, now? How do you spell that?"

She took a deep, controlled breath. She found her balance and her color improved. Her voice trembled. "Let me see his body. I'll have to see it soon, anyway. I'm his only next of kin."

I held up my hands again. Well, one hand and one notebook, anyway. "Look, ma'am, this is a crime scene. I only just got here, and I can't move the bodies until I go through procedure." In hindsight, that "procedure" argument was weak. Miss Carroway ploughed right over it.

She stepped one pace forward and glanced sideways at body number one. Lines appeared between her brows for a second. "That one's first name is Uwe. He was an Ottoman[1] loyalist in the War." Then she gave me the eye. A fierce eye. A wild eye, like an eagle. It was a look that promised she would take her talons and rip through me if I stood in her path. With precise diction, she said, "I will step carefully. Let me see!"

Somehow, although I had the badge and the authority, I found myself nodding. I stepped to one side. She walked by me to look behind the desk. I heard the

---

[1] The Ottoman Empire fought the Allies in the Great War.

catch in her throat as she choked on the words. "Yes. It's him."

I found my lips making strange sounds. "All right, ma'am. Thank you, ma'am."

She averted her eyes from her father's body and turned back toward the door, lurching a little. She didn't look at me as she passed, but she pointed to the contract on the desk. "You'll find that that's all fiction. It was an excuse to get in the door. Darko or his hirelings are long gone, now."

Miss Carroway seemed to be under the impression that our interview was over. She stepped over body number one and through the gaggle of gawking geese.

I chased her. "Wait a minute, Miss Carroway! Tell me about this Uwe and this Darko Dor."

She paused by the reception desk. She put a hand on it and turned to look at me, her eyes twin pools of desolation. "I thought Darko Dor was dead, until I read the letter tonight. He was Minister of Technology of the Ottoman Empire. Uwe was just a guard. That was years ago, obviously."

"What letter?"

"Oh. Here." She extracted a folded piece of paper from a pocket on her sleeve. "My father's last letter."

I took it.

"Thank you," I said. It seemed the thing to say. "Look, where can I reach you, in case I have questions?" Oh, yes. I would have questions.

"My father's house on Bay Shore Drive. Good night, Lieutenant."

"Good night."

I watched her. She hopped into a newer model roadster. She handled the gears clean. No grinding. It wasn't until after she whisked out of the parking lot that I realized I hadn't introduced myself.

How had she known my rank?

I started smelling *eau de rat*.

The dame steamrolled right over me and gave me the name of the murderer, just like that. It was too pat. Did I just get played for a sucker? My cheeks flushed hot and I ground my teeth.

So I hurled some orders around. Loudly, with emphatic stabs of my finger. "Call the coroner! We'll need two autopsies. We're going to match bullets to guns. Russel, you check at the hospital to see if that secretary guy's gonna live. Smitty, get on guard. No reporters. No lawyers. I need to finish with the bodies and the scene."

They scurried, except for Bill. Or maybe Bob. I frowned at him. "What?"

"Uh, the phone call from earlier, Lieutenant. It was from Grant Carroway's house. The operator said it was a woman's voice."

"Oh. All right. Good work ... uh ... officer."

Bob (or Bill) looked pleased at the compliment.

I went to work. I riffled through the contract. Only the first page even pretended to be about shipping cargo. The rest was gibberish. Fiction, like Cecilia Carroway said. "The doll's a regular know-it-all," I muttered.

I looked around for anything else out of place. The knee-brace body's pockets were all empty, but he had a knife up his sleeve. The president's body had a card case for business cards, a wallet, some keys, some loose change. I liked my card case better than his. Mine was shiny metal. My angry flush had cooled. Taking care of business helped. Having a better card case than Grant Carroway helped.

In the executive's drawer I found paper clips and pens and a few draftsman's tools. Behind a little box of shells for his snubnose hid a well-handled little journal. I fished it out.

Carefully glued and labeled snapshots filled the pages. A young woman in last-century clothes gazed at me with a speculative half smile. The label read, "Amiti on the set of Summer Crown. 1899. Already in love."

"Big eyes on that doll," I grunted. The image niggled at the back of my mind. I thought I'd seen that face before.

The next photo showed a young Grant Carroway with his arm around the same girl. She wore an Indian sari and one of those little jewels, a bindi, between her eyebrows.

I flipped faster. It became predictable. Meeting. Courtship. Marriage. Blah, blah, blah. I stopped at a picture of Amiti that showed her on a movie set, with cameras and lights. "Huh. Well, no wonder she looks familiar. Get with it, Lucy. She's a movie actress."

Inevitably, the last pages held baby pictures. I read, without surprise, "Cecilia Carroway, born at sea."

Chapter 3

By the time I got a bowl of chowder, it didn't appeal. I pushed the potatoes around with my spoon for a while, then I pushed the bowl away.

Jim Ross, co-proprietor of Ross's Sharkbite Diner, looked insulted. "What's the mattah, Drew? You off yoah feed?"

"Nah. New murder case. Thinking about the ins and outs. I bet the dame did it, though."

"Murder? Dame who?"

"The daughter. Read the papers tomorrow, Jim-Ross. Nine times out of ten, homicide's a family matter."

"Well, at least I know who done it."

I plopped my hat on. "I gotta drift."

Ross rubbed at his whiskery chin.

I slid off the stool and stalked out. It was late. The drizzle had become rain, but the wind had died down. After a few cranks too many for my back, I persuaded my Model T to start. When it's cold, just adjusting the choke doesn't cut the mustard. I have to tighten the spark plugs to get the engine to turn over.

I putt-putted over to Bay Shore Drive. Carroway's house was one of a row, each with a little slice of beach and a little pier. Fancy. A few were for sale, but nobody much was buying these days. Times were tough.

I didn't know which house was his, so I looked for

a roadster parked out front. The dame's car. Sure enough, I spotted it in the dim streetlight.

"Only police detectives and cat burglars are up past midnight in this part of town." I killed the engine and stepped out into the chill and wet. I drew my collar up and surveyed the Carroway residence. The lawn undulated between borders of tasteful shrubbery. No trees blocked the harbor view.

I half expected a party to be going on. If she did the deed, she might be celebrating. But quiet reigned. Smoke rose from the chimney and firelight leaked out the picture window. Blatantly, I snooped. I snuck up close and peered in. I muttered, "If I weren't me, I'd arrest me for being a peeping Tom."

The unsteady orange of the fire illuminated her, stretched full length on the floor. Long legs trailed from a plain housecoat and ended in flat shoes with rubber soles. Several framed pictures lay scattered around her, but she stared into the flames. If I were a painter and I painted this picture, I'd name it "Loneliness."

Drizzle dripped from the rim of my hat. I turned and squished off through wet grass. A hint of streetlight glow turned an impenetrable night into mere gloom. Slow and noiseless like a good sneak, I padded around to the back of the house. I could barely make out the landscape downslope. A pier stuck out from a strip of sandy beach. A barely perceptible dark blob might be a boat, tied at pier's end.

Suddenly, a back window lit up with electric light. I blinked. The rays from the lit window revealed a guy, hunched over next to a bush, working on something. He looked up.

Don't see me. Don't see me.

He froze. He'd spotted my silhouette.

Damn.

I barked, "This is the police! You better be a real close friend of the family, pal."

He stayed crouched, fussing with something that clanked metallically. A tackle box, maybe. His big, lumpy nose poked out from under the brim of his hat. "Sure, sure, Officer. I'm a friend," he said. The trouble was, he said it in a Jersey accent. I could accept a Hyannis accent, or a Nantucket accent. Even Province-town or Plymouth in a pinch. But Jersey?

I clomped forward. "Stand up. What's your name?" I had an electric torch. I dug it out of my coat pocket.

He snapped his metal box shut and stood up in a hurry.

I got my electric torch turned on.

Big, lumpy nose. Eyes set close together. Acne pits. Blond hair. Large fists, with scars on the knuckles. The fists in particular I noticed, because the goon swung one at me. I jerked back, so he only grazed my jaw.

The momentum of his swing spun him around a quarter turn and put him off balance. I clocked him with the electric torch.

With a satisfying crack, shattered pieces of glass sprayed out. The moment of illumination ended as the light bulb sailed off into the air. The batteries clattered against the side of the house.

The back porch light on the house snapped on. The potato-nosed goon transformed into a sharp silhou-ette. The silhouette howled and clapped a hand to the side of his head. His hat spun off to lodge in a bush. A moment later, he balled up a fist and loomed over me, a vengeful, brawny shadow.

The ineffectual remains of my electric torch dangled from my fingers. I wondered where my gun was. Maybe hung over the back of my chair. Maybe in my desk. It wasn't strapped to me, that's for sure.

I expected him to start pounding me like the heavyweight champion he resembled, but he whirled and grabbed his metal box instead. Continuing the same smooth motion, he accelerated downhill toward the beach like a sprinter out of the starting block.

"Stop!"

He didn't.

Cecilia Carroway came out the back door, still in her frumpy housecoat. She squinted at me. "Lieutenant?"

But I was in motion, running after Mr. Potato Nose. "Not now, dollface!"

I pride myself on keeping trim. I can keep up with the beat cops and rookies just fine. But this blond bruiser was something special. His vague form and his thudding footfalls receded, try as I might to close the distance.

As grass turned to sand, I heard a voice next to my ear. Cecilia Carroway said, conversationally, "Was he trespassing?"

I glanced over. "Miss Carroway! Get some clothes on!" She wore something pale that hugged her skin. A union suit, maybe. She must have shucked off her housecoat and joined the chase.

She and I pounded onto the first few planks of the pier. At the opposite end, a motor revved.

"He's got a boat?" I wheezed between gulps of air.

The shadowy form of a motorboat moved straight

out into the harbor, slowly at first.

Miss Carroway said, "I can catch him!" She accelerated toward the end of the pier, blowing past me like I was standing still. She looked as if she intended to leap into the air and land in the departing boat.

But before she had a chance, there was a flicker of motion from the motorboat. An arm moved in an arc. A metallic glint resolved into a spinning airborne tubular shape. The heavy object clattered onto the pier, trailing smoke.

Miss Carroway braked hard. She planted her feet and twisted.

She dived backward, right into me. I didn't have time to dodge, and she hit me like a pile driver. The impact drove the air from my lungs. Stars of pain sprinkled my vision. My feet left the wooden surface. We flew through the air off the side of the pier, heading toward the water.

I flailed as I fell; an improvised sonnet in semaphore describing the boundless depths of my indignity.

A flash of light filled the world.

For a crystalline moment, the scene popped into vivid detail. The wavy surface just below me gleamed. Cecilia Carroway flew, arms wide, legs together, toes pointed, a creature of the air. I could almost count the stitches along the seams in her union suit. My hat followed in last place.

A throb of thunder vibrated my bones and smashed at my ears.

A giant, invisible hand slapped me into the cold, cold water.

I was under for only a moment. Bubbles of air in my coat buoyed me back to the surface. Hissing splinters of wood fell like jagged rain, and then a wave of water covered me, spinning me over and over.

I can't swim.

I couldn't breathe, anyway, not after that gut punch Miss Carroway dealt me.

The clammy, watery dark closed over my head. It was my worst nightmare. It was the end.

Chapter 4

It wasn't the end. My collar tightened upward. My coat snagged on my underarms. Soon, I cruised through the watery chill, free air caressing my face. A moment later, my heels dragged on sand and the unseen force laid me out on the beach.

I blearily looked up at the short-haired outline of Miss Carroway's head.

"What's going on?" she said, her voice sharp as a thorn dipped in lemon juice. "That was an Ottoman GK-14 grenade! Who was that man?"

"Muh ... muh ..." I had no breath.

"Well, he's long gone, now." Her vague outline looked out to the harbor.

"Poh ... tay ... toe!"

"Lieutenant, you appear to be short of breath. I don't blame you. You lead an exciting life!" The note of admiration in her voice sounded genuine. "I never thought about law enforcement as a career. One would need an eclectic mix of talents to be a detective."

"Grenade?" I finally managed to speak. The paralysis in my diaphragm eased off.

"Yes, Mr. Lucy, a GK-14. War surplus, no doubt. Powerful little thing. Put a ten-foot gap in our pier!"

I thought that over as I sat up, waterlogged, cold, gut-punched, and with ears ringing from the explosion.

"Where's my lid?"

"Keep track of your own hat, crotchety ingrate."

I struggled to my feet. My overcoat weighed a metric ton. Gallons of water sluiced off me as I stood. The whitish shape of Miss Carroway waded in the water just offshore in front of a dim outline shaped like a pier with a ragged, smoking bite taken out of it.

My soggy hat hit me in the face, a splodgy missile of poor opinion.

I fumbled the hat three times before I finally got a grip on it.

"Stop playing around, Lieutenant! Who was he? Why was he here?"

A hand supported my elbow, guiding me uphill. I grumbled, "I don't know who. I don't know why." I twisted my elbow out of her grip and determinedly squelched my way toward the house and its porch light. I left a seawater trail up the beach and onto the grass.

Miss Carroway persisted. "You don't know? Then why are you here at all? It's well past midnight!"

My spine straightened. My jaw tightened. "I'll ask the questions, if you don't mind."

"You just *happened* to be here in time to catch a prowler armed with Ottoman leftovers? I don't appreciate being left in the dark, Lieutenant."

We arrived at the lit porch. I glanced at her. She was a proud flow of muscles, wetly gleaming with rain and seawater. I was used to seeing Shetland ponies. I wasn't prepared for a thoroughbred. I wrenched my eyes away. "Would you consider getting dressed, Miss Carroway?"

"You lack credibility as a fashion critic, Lieutenant.

At least the dunk in the Atlantic washed the chowder spill off your lapel. Why won't you tell me what's going on?"

"Shh. I'm looking for clues." I poked around behind the bush where Mr. Potato Nose had fussed with his metal box. There was an impression in the mud of something rectangular and lots of indistinct footprints. I picked up my scattered torch batteries and stuffed them in my clammy coat pocket. I picked up Mr. Potato Nose's hat.

"You're playing dumb," she said acidly.

I rounded on her. Thankfully, she had donned her blobby housecoat. "Look, toots. I'm as in the dark as you. Some guy with a big nose was here with a toolbox, a boat, and a grenade. That's all I know."

"So you say. Parenthetically, it was a closed metal case with several fasteners. More like a metal suitcase than a toolbox."

Smug, superior Jane[2]. I mentally counted to ten before saying, through clenched teeth, "You know anybody with a big, lumpy nose and some pock marks on his cheeks?"

She gave me a cold stare of exceptionally high quality. It made me feel about an inch tall. "No."

"That makes two of us."

"Then there is no point in keeping you. Good night, *Lieutenant*."

"Yeah, yeah. Good night …" My jaw worked. I spit out, "… Miss Carroway."

I turned and stomped off. My seawater-heavy clothes slowed my pace to a lumbering shuffle as I

---

[2] Woman.

splashed through the lawn to the street. I shivered.

"Arrogant broad," I muttered.

By the time my Model T got me home, I was shivering so hard my teeth chattered like an Underwood Number 5 typewriter.

Chapter 5

The next day, I took Mr. Potato Nose's hat to the P.D. That one rookie with the round face was hanging around. I can't stand an idle rookie. I thrust the lid into his hands.

"Look, here." I pointed to the lining. "It's faded, but we got initials, F. P., or maybe E. P. With luck, they're his. It's a damn big hat size. He's blond or light brown, hair real short. He's over six foot, strong, and fast. He's got a big, lumpy beezer and some acne scars. Look over the wanted posters and see if you can get a match."

"Yes, sir, Lieutenant!"

The kid saluted and skipped off.

I made some phone calls, mostly about Cecilia Carroway. She sat at the top of my suspect list. The bottom, too. I'd bet my collection of *The Black Mask*[3] that "Darko Dor" would vanish in a puff of smoke like Aladdin's genie. I could think of a motive easily enough. Grant Carroway had been rich. Very rich. If the Carroway dame had even a little money, she could hire a hit. Times were hard. There were plenty of shady guys for hire. Easy to hire, for example, some egg to toss a grenade or two to get the police chasing red herrings.

Nobody returned my calls right away.

---

[3] A comic book series featuring mysteries.

I got something from Marge, though. She came out of the radio room for a donut and I accidentally said hello. She looked at me like I was a bug. "You feeling all right, Lucy?"

"Um. Medium. Say, if her name is Cecilia, why do the papers call her Ace Carroway?"

"You ain't heard of Ace Carroway? Good gravy. She's only the most famous fighter pilot of the Great War."

"What about the Red Baron?" I protested.

"He was famous, too, but never mind. You musta just read about the war in comic books. Hold still." She took a corner of a napkin and dabbed at my chest. I squinted down to see what she was up to. Oh. Donut jelly on my shirt.

"So, what do you know?" I asked Marge.

"No proper gossip. She don't talk to newshawks. But she was a war hero, a double ace. And then she turned spy or something and stole a secret Ottoman airship."

Marge looked at me expectantly. I stared blankly back.

"Lucy! Good gravy! It made headlines. It was a ray of hope in dark times."

I grunted. "All right. If you say so. That donut for me?"

"Get your own."

I mulled over what Marge said as I putt-putted a few blocks over from the P.D. to a dive called The Dumpling. This had nothing to do with the case, just a leftover chore. I knocked at the shabby door. Some paint flaked off, but I got no answer. As expected. It was daytime and The Dumpling was a bar. It wouldn't open for hours. Part of the settlement of the case of *Massachusetts v. Squeezer* required the police to do surprise inspections, so here I was. I had all the keys. Front door, back door, inside doors, and roof door. I let myself in.

My nose wrinkled. "Less sick-up smell, today. The Dumpling's coming up in the world. Watch out, Copley Square[4]. New competition." I flashed my shiny new electric torch around the barstools and tables and the house band's drum kit. I checked behind the bar for hard liquor[5], but I didn't see any. I went upstairs. The rooms were unlocked. Good. Mostly bare. No beds or couches. Great. Inspection over. Quick like I wanted it. I left a calling card and let myself out.

My next stop was New Mercy Hospital, pride of Hyannis. Glass doors opened onto a gleaming reception lobby. I flashed my badge at the nurse. Grant Carroway's secretary's name was Randall Mendes. They'd extracted two bullets from his back last night, and now he was asleep. The nurse dangled a sealed envelope in front of me. "Doctor Huffman said to give this to the police. It contains the bullets they extracted."

That put me in a good mood.

"Well, thanks! That's half my mission, here. The other half's Mendes. Can you let me know when he's awake? Here's my card." I may forget my gun from time to time, but I usually remember my card case. It was nicely made. Stainless steel, in fact.

I turned to go and almost knocked a blind man over.

---

[4]A first-class Boston hotel.

[5]During Prohibition, potent liquors like whiskey were illegal.

He had a white cane and dark glasses and a suit so rumpled it looked like the ground in a Chicago feedlot. He was short but solid. The collision made him take a step back.

"Jeez! Sorry!" I said.

"It is not problem," he lisped in some kind of Eastern European accent. "Tell me. Where is reception at hospital?"

"You're there already, pal. Two more steps forward." I cleared the path for him.

I paused to transfer my card case to my breast pocket, where it belonged. I overheard the blind man say, "I need see Carroway Shipping secretary. My cousin. What room number, please?"

The nurse filled him in. "Mr. Mendes is in room 12, sir, but he is not seeing visitors yet. You'll have to come back. Visiting hours start at four."

I was on my way by then, but I heard the blind man answer, "I vill come back."

And then I almost collided with *her*. You know who I mean. She wore a snappy overcoat and matching hat.

"Miss Carroway," I said.

"Lieutenant. Good morning. Mustard spill replaced by donut glaze, I see."

Her cool alto tones gave me the feeling she wasn't all that glad to see me. That put her in the same category as all the other dames I knew. I sniped back, "I've got more depth than you think. Tomorrow, it might be coffee stains."

"I read in the newspaper that Randall was injured." She sounded accusatory, like she thought I should've told her about Mendes last night. Subtle dark circles under her eyes told me she probably didn't get much sleep.

The blind man tap-tapped his way past us and back to the door. He ticked like a walking metronome. Irritating. At least the sound faded quickly as he found the door and pushed through.

I said, "He'll make a full recovery, they think. He's not awake yet, though."

"I see. Thank you. I'm glad they are optimistic. His family's all in Puerto Rico. They probably don't even know, yet," she said with sympathetic softness.

"Well, maybe somebody at the shipping company can get a telegram to them," I said. But something niggled at the back of my brain. I needed a moment to think.

Miss Carroway spoke on. "If they don't, I can remind them later today. I have to see a lawyer next. I dropped by the hospital to see how Randall was."

The Jane was easy to look at, but I had to concentrate. My eyes drifted out toward the street, visible through the glass doors. I raised an accusing finger. "That guy. The blind guy. He said he was a cousin."

Miss Carroway followed my gaze.

The blind man opened a parked car's door. He tossed his cane in then climbed in after it.

My voice rapped out with a steely timbre. "But he sure as hell isn't from Puerto Rico! And blind men can't drive cars!"

CHAPTER 6

I started to bolt outside, but a strong hand encircled my upper arm. Cecilia Carroway said calmly, "The plate is DF40, Massachusetts. It's a brown Vauxhall Cadet with a brand new set of tires. And, he said he'd be back. No need for a car chase if he's coming back."

Miss Carroway was talking sense. "All right. That way, he won't know we're on to him." The blind man's car pulled out. It disappeared in seconds. I smiled wolfishly. "It's gonna be an interesting interview."

I dug around for my notepad and pencil stub. "Uh, Vauxhall Cadet. Brown. New tires. What was the plate?"

"Massachusetts DF40. So you do a lot of interrogations and interviews in your line of work. All part of building a case. Interesting."

"Just like the movies, except I'm better looking."

"And oh, so modest."

"It was a *joke*, dammit!"

I slapped my notebook shut and turned to Miss Carroway in some heat. But she didn't look like she was trying to get my goat. On the contrary, she looked at me with guileless sincerity. "Lieutenant. Do you have a gun?"

I narrowed my eyes. "Yeah, somewhere. Why?"

"Just thinking about fair play, Lieutenant. They have guns. You should, too."

"They? They, who?"

31

"I wish I knew, Lieutenant, I wish I knew."

My job was to investigate my prime suspect, so when she departed, I followed. Thankfully, my Model T started after only a few cranks. Keeping well back, I followed her roadster away from the hospital. My cranky flivver[6] barely kept up. Fortunately, she didn't go far. She parked at the downtown courthouse. A man in a business suit met her with a formal handshake. A lawyer, for sure. So that detail checked out. I'd keep trying, though. I'd catch her in a lie eventually. Darko Dor, Shmarko Shmor.

I drove back to the station. I passed The Dumpling bar on the way. A guy in paint-spattered coveralls scraped peeling enamel off the front door. About time. That shabby eyesore was a drag on property values.

At the P.D., the bouncy rookie met me at the front door. "Lieutenant! Lieutenant!"

"What's your story, morning glory?" His name — I squinted at his badge — was Smitty. He was all right, for a rookie. I wish his face would sort of deflate, though. He looked like a chipmunk storing food for later.

He said, "Fabian Pugsley! The hat belongs to Fabian Pugsley!"

I squinted. I scratched behind my collar. "Uh, rings a bell."

---

[6] A Ford Model T.

"Lieutenant! He's the bank-bomber! Remember Philly and New York? He'd blow a hole in the vault to get in."

"Oh, yeah. Him. He's been quiet after the Wells Fargo one."

"Yes, sir! Their vault—"

I finished for him, "—stayed intact. And Pugsley escaped by running. Outran ten police cruisers. He's got a nickname, right? Fleet? Fleet Pugsley. Last sighted at Belmont Park horse race track, where he bet two grand on a long shot and lost the whole wad."

Smitty smiled ecstatically. "Yes, sir! He's on the most-wanted list! And he's here in Hyannis!"

"That's true. We've got him for blowing up a private pier in Hyannis Harbor. Prosecution guaranteed."

"Oh, swell!" He looked at me adoringly.

"Listen ... guy. Why don't you take a stroll around the block and see if you spot him. Just think if you did, huh?" I winked.

"But. Oh! Yes, sir!" The chipmunk zipped away in less than an eye blink. Chipmunks do that.

I snuck past Marge and decanted a cup of stale joe. I shut the door to my office and brooded.

The coroner delivered his report around noon. I did the bullet accounting after lunch. The bullets in body number one came from Mr. Carroway's snubnose pistol, but only one Luger bullet made it into Carroway. The other bullets in Carroway were .45 caliber. The bullets in Mendes were also .45 caliber.

I smoked my way through three cigarettes. Other phone calls came and went. I got a lead on a character witness living on Nantucket. He knew the dame. I jotted down the address.

I got some dope on the dame's finances. On the face of it, she was swimming in lettuce. She owned her own company, Carroway Propulsion. It made airplane propellers. You never knew, though. Bad habits could get anybody. Drink. Gambling. You name it. One big slip and you're in the poorhouse.

Russel tracked down the brown Vauxhall Cadet. It was rented up in Plymouth two days back under the name James Baker.

Baker. Right. If that was his real name, I'd eat my badge.

I kept my door cracked and spied on the coffee pot. When Marge made a fresh pot, I tiptoed out to snag the freshest mugful ahead of her.

Just as I whisked my purloined java into my den, the hospital called. Randall Mendes was awake. I told the fresh cup of joe in my hand, "Fate has not been kind to you, my steamy friend. Your moment of glory has passed you by. By the time I get back, your perky attractiveness will have faded into the dregs of flat, bitter obsolescence." Don't get the wrong idea. I don't usually talk to my coffee. I just felt literary at the moment, thinking about Nantucket and White Whales. *Moby Dick* would make a great comic.

When I laid my hand on the door handle of my car, I groaned.

I plodded back into my office and strapped on my gun.

I told the cup of coffee, "Don't get your hopes up, now! My reappearance is but a cruel, ironic twist on an already-tragic story. You will die, my roasty friend, without ever having made contact with my lips."

Marge eyed me as I passed the radio room.

"Who're you talking to, Lucy?"

"You can have my coffee, if you want it." I jerked my thumb back toward my cubicle. "It's untouched."

Maybe that mug of java would get its destined consummation, after all.

Chapter 7

At the hospital, I found room 12. I wedged the door open and glanced around the sterile space. Two beds, one empty, some medical carts on wheels, a few chairs for visitors. Mendes, a handsome kid with neat black hair, had fallen back asleep. "Mendes. Wake up."

He didn't.

That was fine. I had some thinking to do. For example, what information did I want to get out of the blind man? I wanted to know if he helped kill Carroway, of course, but I didn't have a warrant or any concrete suspicion. Sure, he was faking being blind, but that wasn't a crime all by itself.

I sat in a chair by the window.

I guess I'd just bait him when he showed up. Quiz him about his family tree. Make him think I knew more than I did. All I knew so far was the fake name James Baker. His Slavic accent might be fake, too.

I put my suspicious mind to work and guessed more. For example, what if this was a hit job? Blind Baker and Uwe Splint-knees were hired to bump off Carroway, and they did. Carroway managed to shoot one of them, but he was outnumbered and outgunned.

Why was Blind Baker interested in Randall Mendes? Did Mendes witness the shooting? If yes, Mendes could maybe describe the hatchet men. If Blind Baker really was a hit man, though, would he care all that much?

Marge pegged the bull's eye about one thing. I did read a lot of comic books. Suppose Mendes plus a sketch artist came up with a face. In the comics, hit men erased their identities. Having that sketch hung up in police departments was inconvenient, sure. But not worth the risk of doing a second assassination in a public hospital.

And if a hit man cared much, he'd wear a mask. Or dark glasses.

Maybe I had it all wrong. Maybe Blind Baker was an actor who dressed like a blind man for fun and wanted to bring Mendes flowers.

I was missing something.

Time to think it through again. I slumped in my chair.

A soft voice said, "Randall?"

My forehead wrinkled. Really? *Her?* Now? My chair was half hidden behind a moveable screen and a rolling cart. I leaned my head over. It was the dame, all right, dressed in trousers and leather jacket.

"Randall?" she said again, a little louder. The secretary slumbered on. She faced me, seemingly unsurprised. "Hello, Lieutenant Lucy. They said he was awake."

"Miss Carroway. Yeah, that's what they told me, too. Say, since you're here, I've got a few more questions."

"Oh?" Judging by her face, she had suffered a sudden stomach cramp.

"The usual ones. I need you to account for your movements yesterday."

"Oh. Very well," she said stiffly. "I was up at G.

Franklin Airport all morning. Around three o'clock in the afternoon, I flew down here to the Barnstable airport. I'd left my car there. I drove to Dad's house, but only his letter awaited me. The one you have. I called the shipping office, but there was no answer."

"G. Franklin Airport? Oh, wait, I know it. It's up north of Boston in Essex County. Where were you before G. Franklin?"

"Atlanta. And before that, Phoenix. And before that, Los Angeles. I've been traveling a long time, coming back from New Delhi and Nepal."

"Nepal? What's in Nepal?"

"A tutor of mine. My father wished me to visit him again."

"Why? Also, who?"

Miss Carroway's lips tightened in subtle anger. "His name is Yogi Rajanathan. And I haven't completed my course of study with him. Dad thought it important that I finish."

"Fair enough. What subject?"

"Spiritual enlightenment."

I probably stared a bit. "So. You've only been in the country …"

"Four days or so, yes. Only to find—" She didn't exactly choke up and start bawling, but she had to stop talking. Muscles along her jaw rippled. Her chin lifted and she looked at the sleeping Mendes.

"You and your father were close?"

She closed her eyes for a moment and nodded. She looked at me. "He wanted the best for me. No one could ask for a better father."

I leaned forward, intent. "He wanted you to *be* the best?"

For a moment, a line appeared between her eyebrows. "That's about right. Everything he could do to prepare me to excel, he did."

"And you excelled."

"I did my best. Usually."

"Did you two argue, sometimes?"

Ace looked at me coolly. "Yes, Lieutenant, of course we did. As I got older, I had my own ideas on what I ought to be doing."

"Like what? Give me an example."

"All right. For example, when I learned to fly, I didn't tell Dad at first. He wanted me to quit."

"Why? Too dangerous for a girl?"

"Very insightful, Lieutenant. That was exactly his thinking." Her voice gained a hard edge. "I could scarcely believe it! All the tutors, all the university classes. What did all of that mean, if, in the end, I was supposed to stay grounded?"

Her gold eyes seemed almost afire.

"So you argued. Tell me about the Great War."

Her eyes closed wearily for a moment. "You must already know. You're really going to make me say it?"

"Yeah."

"Dingy flatfoot." Apparently, she was so well-bred she didn't cuss. I don't think anybody ever called me a flatfoot before. Far too sophisticated for Chicago. Woodenly, she said, "I enlisted without telling Dad and I lied about my age, but I could pilot a plane. I was assigned to the Ghost Squadron on the French front. My letters couldn't fool Dad for long. When he traced me, he wrote letters. They sent me home."

"You hated him for that."

"No," she said. "No, not at all. I had seen war. That

changed everything. I was frustrated, perhaps."

"You killed, over there."

"I killed."

The two words felt as deep as the ocean. Her eyes and her voice held me spellbound.

She said sharply, "Lieutenant, Randall is not awake. Are you finished with your questions?" I was just getting keen, but she was just getting irritated.

"I'm finished for now, Miss Carroway. They say visiting hours start at four."

"Then I'll come back. Goodbye, Lieutenant."

I watched her exit. She moved fluidly and precisely. She was so *careful*. She seemed so sincere and innocent, but how could you tell if a dame with that much self-control was lying or not?

I slumped back down and half-closed my eyes. I mulled over her alibi. I bet it would check out. She wasn't even in the country when this job was being planned.

Or so she would have me believe. I didn't know what to think anymore. I slumped even deeper in the chair. It was early, still. I heard a clock ticking somewhere in the room. It was mesmerizing.

I drifted off.

But something brought me back. A tingle of air, or a slither of something snaky.

I opened bleary eyes to see two men coming in. They didn't see me right away. Blind Baker came first, looking the same as this morning: dark glasses, white cane, and rumpled suit. He pointed at the unconscious Mendes. A second man followed. Taller and squarer, wearing a light tan suit and a stubbly, ratty blond beard.

"There. That must be him," Blind Baker muttered.

"Check," Stubbles answered. He pulled a knife out of his sleeve and advanced on the comatose Mendes like he did this every day. Like he was about to pay the parking meter.

I stood up. I reached for my gun. "Oh no, you don't," I said, steel in my voice.

Blind Baker turned in a smooth motion and shot me.

Chapter 8

A thud shocked my chest. A sledgehammer blow threw me backward into the window. Glass cracked. I heard my own gun go off.

I couldn't breathe. My legs folded in slow motion until I sat crisscross on the floor.

My eyes and ears kept working, even though the rest of me seemed paralyzed. The wall propped me up. Blind Baker took aim at me again.

Somehow, though, his arm raised up and he shot the ceiling, instead. His head moved backward toward the door, too, followed by his whole body arcing through the air as if the hospital corridor had just inhaled him.

He choked out a strangled gargle as he flew. He landed hard, head first, just outside the door. With him out of the way, I could see the agent of his discomfiture. Messy golden hair atop a leather jacket. Trousers on the bottom. Cecilia Carroway stamped an imprint of her boot sole on Blind Baker's face and he went quiet. With a forward step, she loomed in the doorway, blocking it.

Stubbly, blond beard turned awkwardly toward the door. Bewildered, he bleated, "Huh? What? Beat it, doll!"

Cecilia didn't budge. She stood with flexed knees and a quelling stare.

He menaced her with his knife, swishing it in a circle. She didn't even twitch. He lunged at her.

She moved then, like a cobra striking. She slipped aside to avoid the knife, seized the arm, and pulled, using his own momentum to propel him. He flew into the doorframe and cracked his head against it, hard. It was almost seismic.

He moaned in delirium. The pilot smashed his arm over her knee. His arm cracked loudly. He dropped the knife, fell over, and mewled.

As a hubbub started to buzz in the rest of the hospital, Ace removed a pistol from the writhing Stubbly's shoulder holster. She tossed it and his knife onto the empty bed. She came to me, her eyes intense with deep concern, like the gaze of an angel.

I started to breathe again in shallow little gulps. Pain radiated through my chest. Miss Carroway bent to peel my jacket back, to expose whatever gory mess Blind Baker's bullet had made.

I wheezed, "Don't look!" She'd seen enough bullet holes lately.

Her left eyebrow raised a couple of millimeters. Her lips pursed and there came a low contralto humming, soft and haunting. The approaching clatter of footsteps and excited voices drowned out the melodious sound.

She reached for my chest. "No!" I protested again, and there was a brief jolt of pain.

I blinked tears out of my eyes.

She turned my formerly shiny card case over and over in her hand. It was a mess, now. A bullet had gone almost all the way through it.

I started to mull that over. The more I thought

about it, the happier I got.

"Getting your wind back, yet, Lieutenant? You had me awful worried there for a minute." Cecilia's steady alto voice flowed serenely, but I could sense a bubbly layer of laughter underneath.

People poured into the room. Some exclaimed in amazement about blood and bullet wounds and broken arms and two guys laid out like floormats. Others peppered me with a babble of health-related questions. I could breathe a lot better. Miss Carroway extended a hand to help me up. I took it. She held me steady. She wasn't trembling, but I was.

She told the crowd, "The Lieutenant's fine. He shot the shorter one in the arm. He stopped a murder, I'm sure."

My breathing almost didn't hurt. I worked up a head of steam then bellowed, "Be quiet! Call the station! Have the boys clap irons on those thugs!"

Miss Carroway grinned at me. Awful cheeky, I thought. Then she left me and melted into the crowd. I heard her voice say, "I bet the Lieutenant's got a bone bruise on his ribs or sternum. Maybe a concussion, too. Better observe him overnight."

Did I mention she left me? Well, she did. She just abandoned ship. She left me to the merciless mercy of the doctors and nurses. Ten minutes later, all the patrol boys flocked in so they could fawn and slobber all over me. The doctors wouldn't let me leave until morning. After I pitched a fit, they did allow me to see Blind Baker and Stubbly. They didn't look so scary dressed in hospital gowns and ankle shackles.

In the morning, I went straight to the P.D., rumpled, unshowered, unshaven, and grumpy.

My boss, the police chief, smilingly informed me that Blind Baker was wanted in three states and Stubbly was wanted in four. Gangsters from New Jersey, apparently. He kept shaking my hand.

A rookie came in with the latest newspaper and displayed the headline with a grin. What do you know? I made front page. The chief told me how proud I had made him, and how rare it was for the P.D. to get good press.

To put the icing on the cake, or, at least, the glaze on the donut, Marge came out of the radio room and served us coffee and sticky, O-shaped pastries.

Later, when I got some thinking time, I was less happy. The case was still wide open. Given that she'd saved my life, I wanted to push Miss Carroway lower on the suspect list. But if she masterminded the killing, that's exactly the outcome she'd like.

I hadn't gotten anything back about my Darko Dor inquiries. I still didn't know what Randall Mendes saw or heard. Maybe Blind Baker and Stubbly tried to kill Mendes to keep him from talking, but guesses don't hold up in court. It might add up to a solved case in terms of how, but a blank slate in terms of why. And who.

I jotted "Interview Mendes, Baker, Stubbly, and Carroway" on my notepad. I'd get on that. Right after a shower and a shave.

CHAPTER 9

I found Mendes awake and lucid. He spoke like an English professor except for a Latin lilt to his words. No matter how many times I asked, his story always came out the same, and it always came out real short. He couldn't remember anything about the assault. Not a thing.

What could I do? After a while, I gave up. As an afterthought, I asked him, "Were Grant Carroway and his daughter close?"

Mendes relaxed into a smile. "They were, yes. His wife passed away many years ago. Ace was all he had. He never remarried."

"Who was the wife?"

"Her name was Amiti Rishi. The two fell deeply in love and lived a storybook romance, they say, until the boat accident ended it."

"What happened?"

Mendes lost his smile. "The Carroways left their young daughter with friends in Florida and took a two-day cruise to the Sargasso Sea. But there was a terrible wave and a storm. The damaged yacht barely made it back. Amiti had drowned, and Grant's leg was crushed. Alas! So sad!"

"So he raised Ace by himself?"

"That he did, señor! With a small army of tutors. At the time I took employment with him, Ace was in medical school. Soon, of course, the Great War started and she became a pilot."

"Earned her 'Ace' nickname, eh?"

"Exactly so, señor!"

"What about money? Was Cecilia on some kind of allowance?"

Mendes looked at me uncomprehendingly. "Señor? No, she makes her own money."

"How?"

"Many things, I hear. She plays piano at concerts, and she flies airplanes at fairs. She has a propeller factory. Perhaps other things, too."

"Ever heard of Darko Dor?"

"No, señor."

Blind Baker was still unconscious from the gas they use for bullet surgery. Stubbly was awake, though. I made myself at home bedside. I propped my smug feet up and smiled like the cat that ate the canary.

I checked my notes. "Ah. Gus 'Buttons' Saxonbury. Wanted for aggravated assault in New York, grand theft in Delaware, aggravated assault in Connecticut, aggravated assault in Rhode Island, and, pretty soon, murder and attempted murder in Massachusetts." I looked up at him. He didn't seem very happy. Maybe it was partly the shackles. Maybe it was partly that his arm was in a sling and his head was wrapped up like King Tut.

Or maybe it was that I drove home some truth.

"That's a long list, Mr. Buttons." All of a sudden, I

loved myself. "Mr. Buttons" was even better than "Stubbly" for an insulting nickname.

"They might lock you up in a hole so deep you'll never see the light of day." I punctuated my oratory with a slight pause to let his thoughts percolate. What I really wanted to say came next. "Unless, of course, you cooperate. You're small fry, Mr. Buttons. We want who hired you. So. There you go. Start talking. I have a notebook here to jot things down."

He sang like a meadowlark at dawn in Wyoming with a scenic rainbow backdrop. If meadowlarks sing in thick Jersey accents, that is. "I already thought about dis. I'm gonna spill. I ain't got no friends. No friends that'd spring for bail, anyways." I nodded my head in grave agreement. He continued, "We was hired by dis guy named Darko Dor. Youse gonna ask me what he looks like, but I only saw his lower face. It was da creeps. It's all scars on the left side, like a roadmap. He wears a little goatee beard. He hadda accent. I dunno, maybe Russian or something."

I stared. Darko Dor was real.

I said, "He paid in advance?" I hoped for a no. Let it be a no.

"Yeah."

Damn.

"In cash?"

"Yeah, small bills."

"All right, keep going. What else did you notice? Who said what. All that." My sympathetic vocal tones could coax a scared turtle from its shell.

"There ain't much more. There was only the one meeting. It was mostly arranged already. Henny, the guy with the dark glasses and cane, had some connection to the Darko Dor guy."

I consulted my notes on that. "Henny? Oh, Henrik Blume."

"Yeah, Henny. And we didn't know the other guy. He was Darko Dor's man. We called him Smith. His name was really, um, Goldschmidt. Ernie Goldschmidt." Mr. Buttons sounded unsure.

"Uwe Goldschmidt?" I copied Cecilia Carroway's pronunciation of the name, "Oovee."

"Yah! You said it! Dat's right."

"Uh, huh. So, who shot Carroway full of daylight?"

"Henny, I guess. I was on lookout. It sounded like a shootout for a minute, and Smith was screaming."

"How'd it all start? You three just strolled in?"

"Yeah. After some egg with thick glasses drove off, it looked pretty lonely. We waltzed in. Nothin' was locked."

"Why'd you try to knife the guy here in the hospital?"

Mr. Buttons looked glum. "Henny insisted, on account of him overhearing us talk."

"Talk? What did you talk about?"

"We was just talking, after the shooting was over. I came all the way inside and saw Smith — Uwe — lying there. We talked about how he was dead, and if that mattered or not. Henny said we should leave him. He said we done our part good. Now it was up to the bomb operation to finish the other half."

"Bomb operation?"

Mr. Buttons nodded feverishly. "Yeah, that's what I said! 'Bomb operation?' I said. And Henny said there was another target besides the rich guy we just killed, and they was getting killed by bombs. That's when the sneaky secretary guy bolted. He was under his desk the whole time, I guess. We heard the front door make a noise. We chased him outside and we shot him down. But we got nervous 'cause the shots were outside. Anybody could hear 'em, ya know? So, we jumped in our car and made a getaway. Next day, we saw the newspaper. It said the receptionist guy Mendes didn't die. Henny said we gotta kill him. Gotta kill him on account he knew about the bomb plan."

"Who was the target again? For the bomb, I mean."

Mr. Buttons looked blank. "I dunno. If they ever said, I forgot."

"But somebody connected to Carroway."

"Maybe. I dunno."

I frowned at him. It didn't do any good.

I started over with questions. It's procedure. In a police interrogation, you question all the parts of the story several times and check to see if the story matches each time. I conversed with Mr. Buttons for a solid hour. His story didn't change.

That was a pity. I didn't like his story. Specifically, the part about a second assassination by bomb.

I kept thinking about a potato-nosed bruiser bent over a metal box outside Cecilia Carroway's bedroom. Toolbox, I thought at the time. Maybe I should think again.

CHAPTER 10

Back at the P.D., there wasn't much new. The city clerk had phoned in some financial information on the Carroways. The father's bank account sat not too empty and not too full. No suspicious deposits or withdrawals. His daughter wasn't hurting for dough, either. I scratched financial motives off my list. That left motive pretty murky. Maybe Darko Dor hired the hit. Or maybe Cecilia Carroway hired Darko Dor to hire the hit.

I telephoned Miss Carroway at her father's house. She answered. "Hello?"

"Hello, Miss Carroway. This is Drew Lucy. I've got just a few more questions. Mind if I drop by?"

"I can't, Lieutenant. They're reading the will this afternoon. How about this evening? Come for dinner?"

"Dinner?"

"Yes. Dinner. A customary evening meal. Come at six."

"Um. All right." How could a fella refuse?

She chuckled softly. "See you then. B-bye."

"Bye."

I checked my watch. Only noon? I left the P.D., bought a hot dog, and caught the ferry to Nantucket. Character witness interview. I checked my notepad. "Maxwell Neely, 35 Hulbert Ave., Nantucket."

The weather had brightened up. Merry sea spray

frolicked in a bracing breeze. High clouds dotted the skyways. I wondered what dinner would be.

The pleasant ferry ride ended too soon for me. I hiked uphill and past the lighthouse until I located a neat little cottage on Brant Point. White picket fence. Nautical décor.

A long-jawed man opened the door. Quick eyes darted over a trim little mustache. He leaned on a cane like he needed it. "Yes?"

"Maxwell Neely?"

"Ah, no. I'm Cornelius Bildsten." Bildsten sounded as British as bland scones, despite a Germanic last name. He looked at my badge then up to my face. "Maxwell's not in trouble, is he?"

"No, sir. Routine business is all. I'm Lieutenant Drew Lucy, Hyannis P.D., but call me Drew."

"Maxwell?" Bildsten called over his shoulder. "Business about what?"

"I need some background on Cecilia Carroway."

Another man came behind Bildsten, cocking his head over curiously. "Ace? What about Ace? Come in, uh, Drew, did I hear? I'm Maxwell Neely." Neely spoke more like Kansas than London. He was a little thicker than Bildsten, and an errant lock of brown hair half covered one eye. They showed me in. Neely didn't limp, but one arm hung shorter than the other.

"Tea, Lieutenant?" Bildsten offered.

"All right, sure." Tea is stupid. I can't taste tea. But I was being diplomatic. Sometimes, life deals you tea instead of coffee. You just have to accept it.

We settled in at the bay window. Cape Cod was a lumpy green-brown streak across the horizon. "What about Ace?" Neely asked as Bildsten poured.

"I heard that Mr. Neely knew Cecilia, a.k.a. Ace, in the war."

"We both did!" Bildsten said, settling into a seat stiffly.

"What a flier!" Neely said glowingly.

"Both, eh? My lucky day. So, how did you know her?"

Neely said, "The Ghost Squadron, of course."

"Ghost Squadron?" I had my notebook handy.

"The Royal Air Force Guest Squadron," Bildsten said, "The rubbish heap that castaway pilots from other countries got thrown on."

"Commander Harcourt made it work, somehow," Neely said. "We were both there a few weeks when Ace showed up. In about an hour she got her nickname."

Bildsten nodded. "There was a scramble right after a half dozen greenhorns flew in from Paris. By way of introduction, they ran back to their kites and took off again. We chased down a wing of Ottoman Eindeckers. I got one kill that day, but Ace got two."

Neely grinned. "But her second didn't come easy. It was a head-on collision. Ace came out on top, so the enemy pilot got plowed under. But Ace lost her wheels and broke her propeller."

Bildsten said, "And managed the neatest pancake landing right next to the hangar. I was on the ground by then and I ran over to help. Other than a little wobble in the knees, she escaped unscathed."

Neely took up the narration without pause. "The reason the 'Ace' nickname stuck, though, was a darts game that night. She beat everybody, even Jean-Louis."

Bildsten chuckled. "Indeed so, that first night. It never happened again."

Neely gave Bildsten a wise look. "She lost on purpose, after. I saw her alone with the dartboard one time. One triple-twenty after another. Amazing."

I just looked back and forth between them like I was watching a tennis match. When the volley was over, I asked, "You knew her pretty well?"

Neely shrugged. "I guess. She was all business most of the time. She saved my life at least twice." Neely smiled at his friend. "Cornelius saved hers, once! He dived on an Eindecker when Ace's engine was smoking."

"That was my sixth kill." Bildsten smiled moonily.

"What's the story on the airship?"

"Well, now," Bildsten said, "as it turns out, we two have quite the inside scoop on that."

"Yeah? Do tell."

Bildsten patted his thigh. "I was shot down over Verviers. I crash-landed over on the Allied side of the front line, barely. I was injured in the crash."

Neely patted his own upper arm. "Next day, they shot up *my* plane over Verviers. I made it back to the Allied side of the front before I crashed. I was injured, too. The same day, Ace went down behind enemy lines."

Bildsten took up the narrative smoothly. "We two ended up sharing a room at Royal Brompton Hospital in London."

"We had a good chuckle over the coincidence. My arm was broken in several places."

"And my leg likewise."

"Just as our casts were getting itchy to the screaming point, three new patients checked in."

"We overheard them say the word 'Ace,' so we chatted them up."

Neely nodded. "They had flesh wounds, so they left after a couple of days. But they told us the whole adventure. They labored as slaves at an airplane factory, where Ace sabotaged at least thirty-two experimental fighter planes ..."

"... then trekked across enemy-held woods. They faked an air raid at an airship base. Ace and five men managed to steal an airship the size of an ocean liner and fly it to London."

My neck got a workout swiveling my head back and forth.

Neely said, "It was the X8. You probably know the rest."

I blinked. "Err. No?"

Bildsten said, "The X8 was one of the better kept secrets of the war. The Allies had no idea there existed such a large bomber with such a long range until Ace Carroway plopped one down in the middle of Piccadilly Circus."

"The X8s were only days away from being used. So what would have been a horror for us turned into a horror for them. We, the RAF, I mean, patched up Ace's X8 and bombed Verviers. We destroyed the other dirigibles in their hangars. Then we bombed the front lines and whatever else we felt like."

Bildsten smiled sadly. "And then came the swan song of Major Sinclair."

I blinked. "The what, now?"

Maxwell said, "Did you learn about the war from comic books, Drew? Sinclair fought an Ottoman airship in the X8. Both craft and all hands went down in flames over Mannheim. That poet, Binyon, wrote an ode about Sinclair. The poem made women swoon."

Bildsten said, "It almost made me swoon, too."

I asked, "What about Cecilia? I mean, Ace."

Bildsten shook his head. "They sent her back to America. No medals, no thanks, no recognition."

Neely said, "Cornelius here has a whole box full of ribbons and brass. I think he's going to be knighted."

Bildsten harrumphed. "You would be, too, if America had a king."

Neely told me, earnestly, "It isn't fair! Ace earned more kills than Cornelius, and that was before the espionage! But she was sixteen."

I said, "Got sent home to Daddy. How did she handle that?"

They looked at each other then shrugged at me simultaneously. "Why don't you ask her?"

"I will. One more thing. Darko Dor."

Neely said, "Oh! Of course! That's the other thing that happened with Ace and her friends. She killed the Ottoman Minister of Technology."

Bildsten nodded in agreement.

"*She* killed him? Killed him how?"

Neely said, "A car crash, they said."

I said, "Interesting. And what's a minister of technology?"

Bildsten shook his head. "No, not *a* minister of technology, *the* Minister of Technology. In the highest Ottoman ranks. The Emperor's inner circle."

That revelation scraped some rust off my mental gears. I spoke slowly. "Hypothetical question. Suppose Darko Dor survived that car crash. Do you think he'd have enough spite to kill Grant Carroway, just to get back at Ace?"

"Oh, assuredly!" Bildsten said.

Neely nodded. "We heard he enjoyed torturing prisoners."

Bildsten said, "They say he would join firing squads so that he could shoot bullets into people."

I closed my notebook. "All right. Thanks for the straight dope, gentlemen." I was glad to exit the interview. I can't stand tea.

Chapter II

That evening, I drove over to the Grant Carroway residence on Bay Shore Drive. I changed shirts, first. The hot dog I ate on the ferry had squirted mustard down my front.

I hesitated on the doorstep. Learning that Darko Dor was not only real, but one of the worst war criminals in history, changed things. I had been sure Cecilia Carroway hired the hit, but now that story was shot full of daylight. Maybe she was what she appeared, a young woman who had lost her father and who was kind enough to invite me to dinner.

I hoped so.

A cop on a case, though, shouldn't care. I needed to not care. I told myself to stay tough and knocked on the door.

A short woman in a coat popped the door open. Black hair frosted with gray escaped from under her housekeeper's bonnet. She brushed by me, waving me in. "Go in, officer. Dinner is ready."

I grunted. She walked off and I went in.

The next obstacle presented itself: a lawyer. I could tell even before he opened his yap. He dressed so sharp I felt lacerated. He had a deep tan, black hair, a white smile, and a lady-killer face. If I had a daughter, this was the guy I'd tell her to stay away from.

And why was he here with Cecilia? At that thought,

molten lava bubbled in my gut.

"Hubert Bostock, at your service!" he boisterously greeted in a downtown Boston accent. "You must be Lieutenant Drew Lucy. Such a terrible business. Ace is really torn up, though of course she doesn't let on. Come on in. Amelie was kind enough to make a salad for us before she left."

We strolled into the dining room. Cecilia Carroway strode in from the kitchen, carrying the salad. She wore knickers and a cap, but she looked a lot better in it than any newsboy. Her smile warmed me up. "Hello, Lieutenant!"

"Cecilia."

The table was set for three. I wanted a chaperone like I wanted a hole in the head, but there he was, a slippery fashion plate fresh from the tailor. Hubert Bostock even had dimples.

The fancy salad was dotted with shrimp and Mandarin oranges and those little Chinese crispy things. We ate. I heard a few Grant Carroway stories mistily narrated by Cecilia. I learned that he seldom spoke of his wife, but never remarried. I learned that her father took his daughter on lots of trips overseas. One time, Cecilia lost a spelling bee and her father bought her ice cream and used a fork to shape it like a trophy. He presented it to her like the real thing and she laughed. Another time, girl-Cecilia disassembled the electrical junction box in the house. She bridged hot terminals with her screwdriver, and it blew up in her face. Grant Carroway came running, but he just cleaned soot off his daughter's face and didn't yell. He taught her a few things about junction boxes.

I observed the easy familiarity between Hubert and

Cecilia all through dinner. My mood darkened.

I laid my napkin down and dredged my notebook out of the linty depths of my pocket. I poised my pencil stub. "So. Tell me about Darko Dor."

Cecilia raised a gold eyebrow at me. "Didn't I say already? He was Minister of Technology in the Ottoman Empire during the Great War. Quite a few of the new bombs and airplanes that they had were due to him."

"Don't forget the gas," Hubert added. I blinked. Despite Marge's assertion that I only read comic books, I remembered reading about the Ottoman poison gas. Like a lot of folks, I felt a little sick about it at the time. It was an underhanded, impersonal way to kill. If war ever held honor, indiscriminant killing with clouds of toxic fumes signaled the end of it.

Cecilia said, "And the gas. I assumed he was dead."

"Why'd you think he was dead?" My voice came out gruffer than I intended.

But it was the lawyer that answered. "I'll tell him, Ace." He faced me squarely with his clear eyes and clean-cut jawline. "We were prisoners of war, Lieutenant, Ace and I and four other men. We were conscripted into helping build airplanes for the Ottomans in western Germany. We escaped, after we did a little sabotage. And when I say 'we,' I mean ninety nine percent Ace and one percent the rest of us."

"Bert. Stick to the facts." Cecilia Carroway lifted one corner of her mouth in a lopsided smile at the lawyer then nibbled on a shrimp.

"That is a fact!" Hubert protested. He turned to me. "Darko Dor got sweet on Ace. On the very night we were going to break out, he tried to abduct Ace to somewhere deep into Ottoman territory. He made her drive, and he sat behind and held a gun on her. She drove, but not the way he wanted. She raced so fast that if he shot her the crash would kill them both."

I had my pencil on my pad, but I forgot to move it around.

"Ace ended it by wrecking the car against a tree. She skidded in such a way that the back seat where Darko Dor sat hit the tree squarely. Ace walked away from the crash—"

"Wobbled, more like," Ace inserted.

"—but not Darko Dor. He wasn't moving, and there was broken glass and blood all over. I saw more of that than Ace did." The lawyer sipped water. "And there you have it, Lieutenant. And if you don't believe me, I've got four other witnesses you can call."

"Eh," I hedged, looking at Cecilia, "Is that story accurate?"

Cecilia shook her head in the negative. "Whatever drove Darko Dor was not normal human emotion. Bert said 'sweet on me' but he was being too kind. I doubt Darko Dor knew true compassion."

A fierce look in her eyes dared me to contradict her. I didn't feel up to the challenge. She leaned back. "So, what have *you* learned, Lieutenant? Is it really Darko Dor?"

"That, I can't say," I said. It was true, technically. An officer can't discuss open cases with suspects in said cases.

"I presume those men in the hospital are part of the gang."

"Probably, yeah. Investigation is ongoing." I could have said a lot more. But I didn't. Maybe it was the lawyer sitting there, all perfectly tailored and secret-clubbish. I leaned forward. "Miss Carroway, do *you* have a gun? The one hit squad is under glass[7], but if it is Darko Dor, he might try again."

She replied coolly, "Indubitably."

Hubert nodded placidly. I looked back and forth between their unperturbed faces. "You thought of that angle already, huh?"

Cecilia said, "Yes. Who can tell what goes on in his wormy brain? But if he's alive it's inevitable he'd wish to kill me."

"Eh, one more question. How did you know my rank in the P.D. when you walked in on the crime scene?"

She looked at me blankly. "Your badge was showing next to your mustard stain. It said your name and rank."

I changed the subject fast, before my face could change color. "Check. What's on the agenda for you, Miss Carroway? I got your story, and I got nothing else official that I need you for. I probably won't be calling you again, except as a witness when those rough boys go to trial."

"The funeral is tomorrow," said Hubert Bostock, Esquire.

"I see," I said.

Cecilia reached for a map from a shelf. She scooted the dishes over and spread it out. "After the funeral, though, I think I'll fly around the world."

"Huh?" I said, brilliant, as usual.

She explained, "Well, it was what I was up to, any-

---

[7] In jail.

way, before. It takes a lot of planning. Each leg has to be less than three thousand miles, even with the new Lockheed Flyer. So, figuring about 25,000 miles for the circumference of the earth, that's ten stopover points to complete the trip. At each one, there has to be fuel and supplies, or the journey ends."

An eager light sparked in her eyes as she talked, her finger moving and pointing on the map.

"I'll take off from near here. First stop is Juneau, Alaska. Then Dutch Harbor in the Aleutian Islands. I'll work my way across Japan and China, then over to Africa. I figure it doesn't really count unless I dip south of the equator. I'll do that in Kenya. Then, I'll head north through Europe with a stopover in Iceland. I'll end up back where I started: G. Franklin Airport up in Essex County."

The lawyer said, "I think it'll give Ace time to reflect and meditate. I think that'll be good at a time like this."

Cecilia upticked an eyebrow at Hubert. "What do you mean? I'm coping all right!"

"You are coping admirably, Ace," the tanned young man soothed. "It's just that, if I were you, I'd want a break to think things over."

She looked petulant. The expression was girlish. It made me realize deep down that she was young. She was so brash and self-possessed that you could easily miss the more subtle signs of insecurity. Steamrolling me at the crime scene was a wild improvisation, but she got away with it. Bumping me into the drink to save me from the grenade was lightning-quick thinking. She took risks because she was young and had a lot of fire in her belly. Her risks paid off. So far.

Hubert the lawyer broke into my ruminations, misinterpreting them altogether. "You look a little worried, Lieutenant. But, take it from me, you can't talk Ace out of anything using personal safety as an argument. She's calculated the risks, I bet." He turned to the flyer. "What are the risks?"

She launched into a professorial lecture. "The primary risk is mechanical failure, almost all of that being engine failure. Secondary is weather. A distant tertiary is navigation error. But I've charted my route to be mostly over land, so, really, the risk is minimal. I've made half a dozen dead stick landings with the Lockheed on purpose, so I know how she glides. There's a significant safety risk only if more than one failure occurs simultaneously."

The lawyer grinned at me. I said, "I see your point. Well. Thank you for dinner. I'd best be going."

"Ah, me, too, alas. Here, let me help you with the dishes, Ace!" The lawyer jumped up. And, of course, since he was helping, I was forced to help, too. I haven't washed a dish since about 1910. My smoldering hate for him flamed to new, incendiary temperatures.

CHAPTER 12

Salads are fine and all, but I hadn't had enough grease. I went down to Ross's Sharkbite. The Rosses do grease exceptionally well.

"Jim-Ross," I said, between bites of cubed cod, "suppose you were a small gang of criminals, and cruel fate landed you in squeaky clean Hyannis, Cape Cod. Where would you go to have your conspiracy?"

Jim opened his mouth then immediately clapped it shut again.

"Eh? Spill," I said.

Julie Ross's head appeared in the window to the kitchen. "He was going to say that dive where Squeezer had his girls."

Jim kept his head down and began wiping the counter.

"The Dumpling?" I considered it. It stood out for sure. It was an armpit of a place. A Hyannis embarrassment. "But we cleaned it out less than a month ago."

Jim didn't comment, but Julie said, "Guys still go there. It's still the most likely place to score hard liquor." She looked hard at Jim's profile, her voice going sharper. "Not that Jim-Ross would ever do that, *of course!*"

"You give good advice, Julie."

"Wicked good!" Julie said. After one more crusty

look at Jim, her head disappeared from the kitchen window.

Jim said, "So did the Carroway dame knock off her own dad?"

I had to admit, "It's looking less likely. Still possible, though."

"So much for nine times out of ten."

I gave Jim a sour look. "A guy can be wrong. Say, have you seen a tall egg, built solid, but with a big potato nose?"

"Seriously? He was in here two hours ago. Whatta schnozz."

Small towns. Gotta love 'em. "Did he give a name?"

"Nope."

"Did you see a car?"

"Nope."

"See which way he went?"

"Nope."

"He have any company?"

"Nope."

"Well, thanks for the fish 'n' chips, anyway."

"No sweat, Lucy."

I shuffled back to my Model T. It didn't want to start. My arm got sore trying to crank it up. Finally, I quit trying and gave it a kick in the grill. As I massaged my arm, I thought about the raid on The Dumpling when we nabbed Squeezer. We used the key to the roof door of The Dumpling building. The whole Hyannis P.D. poured into the top while the Yarmouth P.D. guarded the ground floor. Success.

I fished around in the glove box for my surprise-inspection keys. I felt their jingle under a couple of comic books.

"Feeling lucky, Lucy?" I asked myself, tossing the keys up in the air over and over.

Three and a half blocks and a rusty fire escape later, I inserted my key into the shabby roof door. I eased into the blackness of the attic. The upper half of The Dumpling had been a doctor's office around 1900, with a bank on the ground floor. The bank was now a bar. The examination rooms … well, *now*, they ought to be empty and idle.

Thumps of bass viol and mournful saxophone notes leaked up through the insulation. Whatever ape they had playing drums was too loud. I lit a match. In the light I could see roof joists caked with dust. I stole over to the hatch and eased down ladder rungs into the long closet on the second floor.

Low voices came sideways through the closet walls, almost overwhelmed by the bass and drums shaking the floor. I shut my eyes for a minute to get used to pitch black, then I opened them. A tiny glow perched on the closet wall like an anemic firefly. The closet had peepholes.

I put my eye to the glow. The room beyond was bare except for a carpet, a lit chandelier, and two men standing. They regarded a metal gadget with leg-like protuberances held by the one with the big nose. A very big nose. I grinned in the dark. I wanted a piece of Mr. Potato Nose, also known as Pugsley the bank bomber. His new hat looked a size too small. The other guy wasn't such a bruiser. He had his back to me.

I patted myself. Gun present. Check.

Pugsley pointed a limber finger at his metal toy. "See? It's got magnets. They'll stick to the car frame or they'll stick to the body. It don't matter."

"But is it powerful enough to ensure death?" The smaller man softly crooned the hard words. The accent sounded Romanian or something.

"Sure, boss! It'll blow the car and whoever's in it to a million bits. I know my stuff."

There was a pause. The smaller man took to pacing. With his first crisp, military pivot I got a look at his mug. Livid scars crossed and re-crossed the left half of his face in a distorted spider web. He wore a goatee beard. He stopped and leveled a finger at Pugsley. "Very well! But if anything, anything at all goes wrong, abandon the car bomb idea and continue with *my* plan. Do I make myself clear?"

"Clear as a bell, Mister Dor. Don't worry."

"Be exact, Pugsley. I care only about results."

The scarred man gave Pugsley the evil eye for a few more seconds, then he broke off eye contact and headed for the room exit. He was leaving! Pugsley was left holding his magnetic bomb. He assured Dor's back, "I'm careful! Very careful."

I was caught flat-footed, and it was dark, but I had a decent idea where the doorknob was. I palmed my gun. I managed the door all right, and I was in time. I stepped into the path of Dor and pointed my roscoe between his eyes.

"Hold it right there! This is the police."

He stopped. Dark eyes glittered malevolently in the shadow of his hat brim. "What is it that you want? This, it is a free country." His tones of voice were entirely too casual for me. Call me paranoid, but usually a gun and the word "police" garners a more expressive display of emotion.

Pugsley twitched in the background. I told him, "Freeze, Pugsley. You keep holding that contraption right where I can see it." I shifted my eyes to Dor. "We're just going downtown for some questioning. But first, let's go down to the bar. You first. And get your hands up where I can see 'em."

Dor's lips curved in a superior smile, one side pulling at his scars. He didn't move, didn't put his hands up. Also, faintly, he hissed. Not a human sound. It was like letting air out of a tire valve.

I did what any red-blooded boy in blue would do. I cocked the hammer of my pistol back. Click-click.

"You better—" I began. I blinked. There was an odd, cloying scent in the air. The dim world of the upstairs of The Dumpling dimmed darker to my eyes. The hiss continued. My gun hand wavered.

Dor's hand appeared out of his pocket. He clapped a sort of metal mask over his mouth and inhaled. A muffled voice said, "I do as I please. Darko Dor takes no directions from a mere policeman!"

My muscles wouldn't obey. My gun arm sagged. A black fog clouded my eyesight. I fought to stay on my feet.

Darko Dor's voice came, more distant. "The window. Get out by the window, Pugsley. Move! Go before the gas reaches you."

"But—!"

"Drop it! Drop it and go! Stupid Yankee."

I had a hazy impression of the shadowy form of Darko Dor reaching to his boot. He unsheathed something long and silver. My eyes went black. My skin was all tingles. I tried one more thing. I squeezed my finger. My trigger finger.

There was a pop sound. The tingly shock bucked in my hand and traveled up my arm. I vaguely sensed the floor rise up. Distantly, I heard the heavy sound of my boneless body meeting it.

Chapter 13

Voices babbled. They babbled from the far end of a long culvert, echoing, scrambled.

"Shut up," I said.

"He's coming to!"

"Beverly? Got those smelling salts? Put them under his nose."

"Shut up," I beseeched.

Then white-hot iron poured through my nasal passages. My head was on fire.

"Ow! Ow! Stop!" I opened my eyes. About seven heads looked back, arranged like daisy petals with me at the golden center. I figured out I was flat on my back on the floor, looking up.

"Whew, he's all right!" I recognized the curls on Big Beverly's head. She owned The Dumpling. She didn't like owning it, but this was a lousy time to sell a run-down bar. She didn't go to jail like Squeezer did because she was on a long vacation in Florida while he turned her bar into a house of ill repute. Every time she said she might come back, Squeezer sent her another payoff check. She stayed at the beach.

"I'm awake! I'm awake! Put that bottle away, Beverly!" The fire in my head gradually faded. "They got away, didn't they?"

"There's nobody here but you, Lieutenant."

"Why'd you shoot the floor, Lieutenant? You put a

hole through the snare drum!"

"I got your attention," I growled, "and improved the quality of music, all in one easy step." I sat up. With my head clearing, I felt other pains. Bruises flared. A couple of places on my neck stung.

A more distant voice said, "There's a funny thing by the window. It looks like a dog robot."

I struggled to my feet. "It's a bomb. Don't touch it! Call the P.D."

"Already did, Lieutenant."

I raised my hand to my neck. My fingers slipped on warm wetness, slightly sticky. As I stared at the crimson staining my fingers, the drummer boy told me, "Go easy there, ya nutty egg. You're bleeding. You're bleeding a lot."

It turned into another late night at New Mercy Hospital.

"You were skewered," the doctor told me. "You are one lucky chump. Phineas Gage has nothing over you."

"Phineas who?"

"The man who got a rod pushed through his head and didn't die. What do you read instead of newspapers? Comic books? Anyway, you got impaled through the neck with a narrow blade. Something like a rapier or stiletto."

I rubbed at my new neck bandage.

The doctor continued, "The blade entered to the

right of your trachea, angled left of your carotid artery, and somehow missed your spinal column before emerging out the back. You escaped with a mere flesh wound."

"Lucky Lucy, that's me." My lips felt numb.

The doctor looked at me gravely. Eventually, he said, "Well? What happened?"

I looked at the wall. My coat hung there, all red-rust blood around the collar and a couple of horizontal stripes of bloodstain across the middle. I didn't remember being stabbed, but I could imagine the uncaring thrust. Darko Dor wanted a quick death for me before he escaped with his henchman. He pulled his thin assassin's knife. In and out, he punched it through my neck. He hastily wiped it on my chest. I bet he smirked under his gas mask before running for the window and fire escape beyond. It should have been curtains for me. But I felt my lungs pumping in and out. Beyond any reasonable expectation, I was still breathing.

And now the doc wanted a story. I turned haunted eyes on him. "How'm I supposed to know?"

The doctor wasn't satisfied, but he saw no medical reason to keep me.

Chapter 14

When I dragged myself out of bed the next morning, it was nearly noon. My neck was swollen and stiff. Every motion hurt. It hurt to drink coffee.

Next on my to-do list was interviewing Blind Baker. I didn't do it. I went to Grant Carroway's funeral, instead. Out of curiosity, I suppose.

I dressed in civvies. I hid my neck bandage under a scarf tied like a gentleman's cravat. I arrived to the funeral late. I slouched into the back of the church and listened. A half dozen people gave speeches about Grant Carroway. I learned he funded an orphanage and donated to hospitals. Several people mentioned that he was a sad man, except when Ace was around. Mostly, they all called her Ace. A few guys in suits talked about how ships he built opened up new shipping lanes and broke speed records.

Cecilia was there, but she didn't give a speech. It was the only time I saw her in a dress. Dark gray with two rows of buttons. Very nice. Regal. She wore a hat with a fishnet veil flowing down over the wide brim. A lot of eyes were on her.

After, we all flowed out in slow motion behind pallbearers and there was a ceremony of interment. A long line of folk paid their respects. I shook my head to myself. If I died, only my dog would be there to mourn me. Except that I didn't have a dog.

"A well-respected fellow, Grant Carroway. Many

will miss him. Alas that I never met him," said a voice at my elbow speaking in a Boston accent. I looked over.

Crap.

The lawyer.

"You never met him?" I said.

"No."

"So, you and Cecilia ...," I said. My yap ran ahead of my brain.

The handsome fellow looked at me sharply, then swung his head from side to side. With a wry, self-deprecating smile, he said, "Ace called me to check on the legal aspects of the will, that's all. We haven't kept in touch very well since the Great War, our little gang of former POWs."

I felt a little glow inside. I felt better about *him*, for sure. I noticed that we both were standing on the outside of the circle, where strangers that didn't know anybody would drift. He wasn't by Cecilia, holding her hand, for sure. Good!

He reminisced, "After the war, I finished my law degree and went into practice. I think Gooper's a professor, now. Boxnard Warburton went from quack to hack. I hear he's very popular on Broadway. Tombstone's an electrical engineer, and Sam's an archaeologist. We send each other a card once a year. It's a shame. We went from saving each other's lives to barely knowing each other."

"Welcome to the grind, I guess," I said.

"At least Ace still has the spark." The lawyer's smile faltered. "Maybe too much of a spark. After talking with her, I'm a little worried."

"How so?"

"Well, after her discharge, I'm not sure she ever patched it up with her father. Ace threw herself into, well, into *achieving* things. She finished her M.D. and started a Ph.D. program in physics. She competed in martial arts contests." He looked at me. "That's like Chinese boxing."

Cancel that part about feeling better about him. Now, I wanted to Chinese box his face to a pulp.

"She patented a new type of airplane propeller. She's a concert pianist. The list goes on and on. Now, it looks like she might be seeking more of the limelight."

"I thought she gave reporters the cold shoulder," I said. I remembered that tidbit from Marge. Marge would be amazed that anything penetrated my skull, I'm sure.

"That has been true, until now. I heard her mention getting a photographer. She even laughingly referred to running for political office. That just scares me."

"Eh?"

"I'm sure she'd be a great governor or the like. I just think it would be a waste amid all her other, greater talents. Being famous goes nowhere in the end, and I thought she knew that. Yah, she used to duck reporters, but I think she's losing her focus."

"I see. Well. What do you think she'll do?"

The lawyer smiled wistfully. "Short term? I think she'll go on her round the world trip. She departs tomorrow."

He said it so sudden, it took a minute to register. Then a voice squeaked, "Tomorrow?" The voice sounded plaintive and whiny. Couldn't have been me. But it was.

The lawyer laughed, but it was a sympathetic laugh that made me think he understood how my stomach had knotted up. "Yah, I think she said tomorrow. As for me, I'll drive back to Boston tonight. I have to prepare a brief tomorrow. The grind, as you said, Lieutenant."

The funeral broke up. I stood in the reception line, and when it was my turn, I shook Cecilia's hand and said, "Condolences."

That was all I did. I wanted to tell her that her father left quite a mark on the world. I wanted to tell her that I was sorry I thought she had murdered her father. I wanted to tell her that Darko Dor was real, and that he'd gassed me last night and then stuck a stiletto through my throat.

It wasn't until I was cranking up my rattletrap of a car that I realized what I wanted most of all. I wanted to ask her out to watch a Silent at the Bijou. That was stupid in a lot of ways, but it was especially dumb if she was going around the world tomorrow.

Henrik Blume's dark glasses, suit, and cane were now State's evidence. His blond buddy was already gone from the hospital. He was in a cage at the P.D.

until the Chief and the D.A. sorted out which order his various criminal trials would be docketed. Apparently, I had shot Blume in the arm about the same moment he shot me in the card case. Then Miss Carroway had pummeled him like a Jack Dempsey thrashing a Jess Willard.

When I got to him, he was sitting up in bed. He held a drink with his good arm, sipping from a straw into his blotchy, purpled face.

I gave him the same drill as his buddy. I told him how bottomless his pits of despair were then offered leniency if he spilled. He wasn't so quick to blab as Mr. Buttons. He kept saying, "I ain't talking, copper!" in a Slavic accent. I hear the cinema thugs all say "I ain't talkin', copper!" in the new talkies they show down in New York.

I kept at him, though. After a while, my punctured neck felt like it was swelled to twice its size, but I orated like a second Lincoln anyway. I painted him word pictures of what the 40th year in prison would be like. I showed him photos of the cute kids he'd never be able to have. I let him feel the softness of the cheeks of all those beautiful dames he'd never get within miles of. I found his tipping point, eventually, and he babbled like a drunk in confessional.

His story jibed with what I knew. Darko Dor hired them to do the killing. Uwe Goldschmidt was the name of dead body number one, and Blume himself had ended Carroway and shot Mendes in the back. I acted bored, writing all that down, like it was drudgery. Pretending disinterest, I asked, "Now, tell me about the bomb plot."

He didn't hesitate. "Uwe told me a little. Grant Carroway vas number one target. Number two target vas Ace Carroway. Uwe hate her a lot. He say she broke his legs. After this job, Uwe vas going next to join whoever vas setting the bomb. He did not say who."

My lips felt numb.

"Did he say where? Did he say when?" I managed to mumble.

"I don't know when, but he say G. Frankfurt Airport." His eyes narrowed in thought. "No, not Frankfurt. G. Frank-something."

"G. Franklin Airport in Essex County."

"That is right. *Ja.*" The assassin nodded.

CHAPTER 15

I raced out of there. I spotted a clock at the nurse's station.

"Two in the morning? Time flies when you're Lincoln."

I hopped in my Model T and putt-putted over to the Carroway residence. I had wanted a new car for a while, but this was the first time I really needed a new car. I wanted speed, but I couldn't have it.

It's a wonder my chokehold grip on the steering wheel didn't leave finger-shaped impressions. When I got there, the house was dark. I ran to pound on the door. Silence. The dark house stayed dark.

I talked to myself. "All right, she's gone. She went to Essex County. That's still in Massachusetts, but way up north of Boston. What does 'tomorrow' mean for a pilot? It's already tomorrow by suitably twisted definitions. But nobody's going to be awake up there at 2 a.m."

Finally, I growled like a dyspeptic pirate and hopped back in my flivver.

The cavalry was coming. At around 30 miles an hour. 35 if I caught a tailwind.

Within half an hour, the vibration started. The Model T started thrumming like the bass viol at The Dumpling. An hour later, it was shaking my teeth out. As I rolled into the outskirts of Boston, something broke loose. The engine roared in futility. The so-called car coasted to a stop. Most of the drive train dragged and bounced on the ground underneath, clanking mournfully. It was 4 a.m.

I got out, kicked the pile of scrap metal that used to be my flivver, and started walking.

I racked my brain. Who did I know in Boston? I wanted to flag down a passing car, but there weren't any. Half an hour of walking later, I found a garage. It was closed, but it had a pay phone.

I dialed "0."

"Operator," came a voice right away.

"Operator. Get me Hubert Bostock, please. It's an emergency."

There was a silence, then the voice came back.

"I have a Hubert Devery Christopher Bostock the Third on Beacon Hill. Is that who you want?"

I blinked once. The lawyer was one of *those* Bostocks? I replied, "Yeah. Yeah, that's him."

I waited.

At long last, I heard, "Connecting you now."

"Hello? Hello?"

"Hubert! This is Lieutenant Drew Lucy from Hyannis. Glad you're home."

"Lieutenant? What time is it? No, never mind that! What is this about?"

"I hope you have a car. Mine broke down. And it's about Ace Carroway. I got a tip somebody is going to put a bomb in her airplane. Or already has. Put in a bomb. Hello? You there?"

"I'm here, Lieutenant. I understand. Tell me where you are. I'll come get you."

"Yeah, it's Mikey the Mechanic on the road to Cape Cod around Boston city limits."

"I know the place. Hold tight."

There was a click sound, then the operator said, "Did you say a bomb?"

"Yeah, you heard right. Listen, would you ring up G. Franklin Airport in Essex County? Tell 'em to ground her plane. I mean Ace Carroway's plane."

"Nobody's going to be there this hour of the morning! Why, it's 4:30 a.m.!"

"Could you just try, please?"

"Sure, mister. Sure, sure. The Beacon Hill Bostocks and now Ace Carroway? You move in rare high circles, buddy."

I sourly mulled that over while the operator rang the airport.

Nobody answered.

CHAPTER 16

I paced shoe-leather off my soles until a two-seat roadster roared up. It screeched to a halt by me in a cloud of dust. I hopped in. It squealed in acceleration before I even shut the door. Hubert Bostock could and did drive like Kitty Brunell[8]. Good. Even if the wild driving bounced me around, I could take a few more bruises.

I told him what I knew as we careened north. I caught him looking at my neck. But I didn't want to talk about that. I re-wrapped my cravat to hide my bandage.

Boston was asleep except for a few milkmen. We made good time up to the New Hampshire border where G. Franklin sits. The sun was thinking of rising when we tore into the grounds.

We drove around the radio shack onto the airfield itself. A flash of light caught my eye.

"What's that?" I blurted.

But it wasn't an explosion. My stomach unclenched, slowly. "A photographer's flash, maybe," Hubert said.

"Go that way."

He drove. A hangar loomed ghostly in the predawn. Above it, a tiny silhouette danced like a mote in the eye of the brightening sky. "Oh, no!" I said. "That's an airplane!"

---

[8] A race car driver famous in the day.

We came to a stop in front of the hangar. A small, sleek airplane sat out front. Three people stood by. Two slouched with hands in their pockets. The third held a camera.

Hubert and I popped out of the roadster. I could hear the fading buzz of the airplane. I growled at the trio of people, "Where is she? Is that her? Is she gone already?"

The trio all looked at each other. One of them said, "What?"

I used what I call my galvanizing voice. It's like my decisive voice, but louder. "Where's Ace Carroway?"

"Yeah, where?" Hubert chimed in.

A fourth person appeared from around the tail fins of the parked airplane. A slim figure wearing a flight suit, cap, and goggles. In a droll alto, Cecilia Carroway inquired, "Looking for me, gentlemen?"

"Cecilia!" My legs went to jelly.

Hubert threw an arm around my shoulder. "Steady, there, Lieutenant!" I could have used some of Big Beverly's smelling salts right about then.

One of the men said, "The plane in the air? That's just the morning mail service."

"What going on?" Cecilia asked.

Hubert's words tripped over one another in his rush, "The Lieutenant got a confession that said they were planning to plant a bomb in your plane, Ace!"

Cecilia's lips compressed to a thin line. She said, "But I've been inspecting the Flyer. If there is a bomb, where could it be?" Her single-engine airplane was all silvery-smooth metal. It had "Lockheed Flyer" and some call numbers painted on the side.

"Uh. Cockpit? Engine compartment?" hazarded

one of the two fellows standing around. Their hands were out of their pockets, now, and they looked nervous. They must work for the airport.

Ace ran her fingers along the wing, then opened up the engine cowl, and peered in. She shook her head. "I've been over both those places. There's no room."

I said, "They might have had a lot of time. All night, maybe."

She looked at me with a smile that warmed me from shinbone to pate. "The Flyer's got a duralumin skin, Lieutenant, but the skin is so tough it's part of the plane's strength. The technique is called monocoque. But there are a couple of access plates. Let's try the easiest one, first."

She turned to one of the airport men. "Abernathy, lend me your screwdriver."

The portly fellow had a whole tool belt. He selected a screwdriver and handed it over.

Ace took it toward the tail and crouched down. She worked to undo an access plate in the skin of the airplane, screw by screw.

The rest of us fidgeted.

"Um. How big a bomb?" Abernathy asked me. I shrugged at him. He shifted his weight from one foot to the other and his forehead grew worry wrinkles.

Ace removed the curved plate. She sat it down and dropped the liberated screws on it. She peered into the shadowy hole. There was a contralto humming sound, soft and haunting.

I quivered. I had heard that sound before, when she had peeled back my jacket to realize that my card case had caught Blind Baker's bullet instead of my heart.

She said, "Abernathy. Wire nippers," and held out

her hand, a surgeon at work.

His jowls shook as he realized he needed to go closer to Ace. Fumbling, he managed to extract his cutter and placed in her waiting palm.

Clinically, Ace said, "It's a bomb. I am going to disconnect the timer. You might want to stand back."

Abernathy scurried away from the plane, sweat gleaming from his face. The photographer and the other mechanic joined him. Hubert and I reluctantly shuffled back a foot or two.

She reached the tool into the hole delicately, like she was trying to catch sunbeams. Her forearm sinews flexed. A soft click sounded. Ace dropped the nippers and slipped both hands in. In slow motion, she removed a lumpy black and red object about the size of a shoe box.

The photographer gasped. "Holy smoke!" He fumbled with his gear.

As the rising sun rosily lit her golden face, Cecilia gently carried the infernal machine a few dozen yards to the grass off the runway. She set it down soft as goose feather down. The photographer chased her, popping off flash powder as fast as he could reload.

The two airport guys looked so wide-eyed they should move to Madagascar and join the lemurs. Bert shook his head. "Unbelievable. Simply unbelievable."

Ace came to me. My heart thumped.

She took my hands and held them both. "Thank you, Drew."

My first try at saying something couldn't get past the lump in my throat.

I tried again, attempting to be gallant. "You're cleared for takeoff, Captain."

CHAPTER 17

Unfortunately, she *was* cleared for takeoff. She put her plane back together, finished her inspection, and then took off for Juneau. We all waved, and we saw her give the thumbs-up as she roared down the runway.

I watched until she was a tiny dot in the sky, and then the dot was gone.

The airport guys and the photographer had already disappeared into the radio shack. I bet they had hot java in there. And they might be on the horn to the police about a bomb sitting on their grass.

Bert clapped me on the back. "I think you should call in sick today, Lieutenant! Come back with me to my flat and we'll take a nap. I'll treat you to dinner. Sound good?"

"Yeah, sure. Sounds more than good."

As Hubert and I walked along, something was nibbling at the back of my mind. I closed my eyes and relaxed, letting the idea take form. Something about knowing human nature.

Then, I got it.

I grabbed the lawyer's elbow and tugged him close. I talked low and fast. "Listen. If you set a bomb, would you just walk away? Or would you wait around and watch and see if it all worked out?"

"You got my attention, Lieutenant!"

"I think there's a guy hiding in the hangar. You go around back and cut him off if he tries to run that way. I'll go in the front. Check me?"

"Check," he said with a carnivorous grin.

We split up. I gave him a half minute to get in position. I approached from the front of the hangar, as out of view as possible. I kept my eyes open.

The hangar was clear in the middle, but untidy everywhere else. Along the walls stood scattered stacks of crates, racks of tools, bins of spare parts, and piles of paint cans.

Movement! I had a fleeting impression that a head ducked out of sight behind a stack of crates and boxes. The boxes formed a row on my side of the hanger about a third of the way along.

I ran for the spot. I tried to run silently. I don't think I managed it, but I wanted to move quickly. I didn't have a plan.

From behind a jumbled stack of assorted shipping crates, a pistol and a hand crept into view.

A bare head with short hair followed. I took a dive, feet first. The floor was slick concrete. I slid at full speed like a base runner dodging a tag. My neck protested with a stabbing jolt of pain.

My feet slammed into the wooden crate hiding the gunman. I kicked hard. I heard a pained croak and a gunshot simultaneously.

The boxes on top started to fall, but I wanted to get at the gunman. I flailed and clawed at the various tumbling cubes, rabid and foaming, tearing a path, any path toward my prey.

I caught sight of a gun and a hand close enough to grab. I clutched frantically. The gun went off again. A deadly whiz whisked by my ear.

A punch to my belly rocked me. I punched back, left-handed. I connected on something bony and I felt him sag. I kicked. My foot struck something meaty and he grunted. He swung a fist. I saw it coming but I couldn't dodge. My jaw exploded and my swollen neck lit on fire. I could see only stars. Mainly by sense of touch I tried to break his gun arm on the corner of a crate as he tried to point the gun at me.

A foot swept my legs out from under me. I landed on my back with him on top. He was strong and heavy as an ox. The pistol got closer and closer to my head. I punched over and over at his midsection with my free hand, but it didn't seem to have any effect.

The gun wavered in the tug of war. I saw right down the black of the barrel.

In the periphery, I caught a silver glint of light.

A hollow thunk sounded. Suddenly, I won the contest with the gun, and the lug went limp on top of me.

Standing over us, Hubert raised a shiny wrench about the length of a forearm, ready to bounce it off the thug's skull again. But one concussion was enough. The man's eyes glazed, unseeing. I shook the gun loose and it skidded across the floor. I heaved the guy off me.

Hubert gave me a hand up. I panted. We grinned at each other and clapped each other on the shoulders. I forgave him his good looks and bloated bank account, then and there.

I kicked the faintly moaning body of the thug until he rolled over on his back. Bert remarked, "Ew. Now, that's ugly. He's either from Jersey or Grimm's fairy tales. Look at that nose!"

"His name's Fleet Pugsley, the bank-vault bomber."

"Wicked. At this rate, you'll single-handedly decimate the population of at-large criminals, Lieutenant."

"Call me Drew."

"Call me Bert."

Chapter 18

I'm about done with this story, but the rest is uglier than Pugsley.

About a week later, a guy came to see me. His suit and hat looked like he slept in them, they were so wrinkled. He found me in my office and shut the door. "Lieutenant Lucy, I presume," he said in a sandpapery voice. He flopped an identification pamphlet on my desk.

I picked it up. "Major Franklin Case, Office of Naval Intelligence. What can I do for you, Major?"

"It's about Darko Dor. He's international, so it falls in ONI's purview. That bird you caged at the airport, Pugsley, he talked. From his information, we brought in his supplier for questioning."

"I'm interested. Keep talking."

"They both mentioned bombs. It took us a little while to sort the stories out, but ..." he trailed off, bushy eyebrows squirming.

"But, what? Spit it out!" You can write on my epitaph that I chewed out a Navy officer and lived to tell the tale.

"Turns out, there were two gangs planting bombs. One here, one in Chengdu, China."

My stomach dropped like an elevator with brake failure.

He continued, "We got on the teletype right away. We told 'em to hold Ace Carroway in Chengdu. We haven't heard back. But I thought I'd better let you know."

"Yeah. Thanks." My lips felt numb.

The major kept talking. I heard about every other word. "This Darko Dor. Word is, he's turned himself into a crime boss. His name's getting known in the underworld. He definitely put out the contract on the Carroway family. He swore revenge on Ace and everybody close to Ace, including friends. But he's careful about covering his tracks. We don't have any leads on his whereabouts, yet. We'll get him, eventually." Major Case smiled, maybe trying to cheer me up. It didn't work.

I mumbled, "Let me know when you hear something, all right? I'd appreciate it."

We didn't hear much. Chengdu finally reported that Ace Carroway had come and gone.

New Delhi? Ace never arrived in New Delhi.

I moped around a while. I think Marge noticed. She yelled less than usual and made me fresh coffee once or twice. That made me smile, and the smile felt good.

I knocked on the door of the radio room.

Marge looked up. "Lucy? Since when do you

knock?"

"Since I started feeling apologetic. Sorry for being a sourpuss. I'll make an honest try to be a little more human from now on." It was strange to hear myself say those words. Stranger still, they felt good to say.

"Aww. Naww. It's all right," Marge stammered.

I grinned and turned to go.

Then I came back. "Marge?"

"Yeah?"

"You free Saturday night? I read in the paper they got talkies down at the Bijou now."

"Yeah, sure, Lucy. Sounds like a kick." Her eyes were like saucers. They were kinda blue-green.

Chapter 19

The Aleutian islands were like a giant's stepping stones plopped in a ragged, west-pointing line. In contrast to the harrowing Canadian Rockies crossing, the weather had cleared. Visibility was infinite. The engine heat plus the sun warmed the enclosed cockpit to a livable temperature. In the calm upper airs, the Lockheed Flyer almost flew itself.

Ace dreamily watched the bright oceanscape, occasionally glancing at the compass. Unbidden, her hand reached to her thigh pocket. A moment later, Ace turned a sealed letter over and over in her fingers. It had been among the will documents.

"Now, I suppose," Ace murmured, her voice completely lost in the drone of the engine. She broke the seal and unfolded the letter.

My dearest daughter,

As best a man can plan for the unthinkable, I hope I have done. If you are reading this, I have passed away. I have updated my will several times, and written a new version of this letter upon each occasion, but this time I am not at peace. I have one more tutorial to impart.

My heart nearly burst when you ran away and joined the Expeditionary. I felt that I would lose you. I felt I had lost you. Paradoxically, that feeling persisted even after you returned safely. You never expressed your anger at me, but I could feel it. I could feel the new distance between us. Rajanathan wrote to me, and I think I understand my mistake.

When you were a child, I tried to give your wings room to grow. I see now that you have grown. I see now that only the wide world can contain you. Perhaps even the whole world isn't wide enough.

I apologize for the metaphorical cage I built around you, my daughter. I hope you will forgive a father for clinging too much.

I am gone. You have my savings and my business interests. But you also have my undying love.

The fleeting days of a life are too few. Mine have run out. Yours? I wish for you to live each hour vividly. Taste the flavor of each minute like a connoisseur. Feel each heartbeat as if it were a victory cry.

Dearest daughter, yours is the purest heart I know.

Fly high.

Love,

Dad

Ace lowered the letter. The compass bearing was still true.

"Oh, Dad!" she said. Her eyes brimmed with tears. Finally, Ace let them flow. The pent-up reservoir of grief burst through the dam. Witnessed only by the sparkling Aleutians, Ace said goodbye to her father.

Days later, after a refueling in Chengdu, Ace flew between Himalayan peaks Kang Guru I and Lamjung Kailas. She ungloved to mark her position and time on the navigation chart. The Lockheed Flyer had an enclosed cockpit, but the high altitude made it bitingly frigid inside. She wore gloves, scarf, and a jacket. Looking at her mark on the map, Ace smiled and murmured, "Well, hello and goodbye, Rajanathan! So sorry to come and go." The weather was unsettled but acceptable. Ace trimmed the ailerons to begin a gentle descent.

In the tail of the plane, nestled among cylinders of explosive, a silent timer reached its appointed hour. A tiny cog inched forward. An open electrical circuit closed. Thermal resistors flared. The explosive powders ignited. From tiny beginnings, the chemical reaction proceeded exponentially. The cylinders disappeared in an expanding blank sphere of fury unleashed. The tail of the Lockheed Flyer was engulfed in superheated gases. The concussion sent metal scraps flying. The rudder flew off backward into space. Shrapnel pierced the cockpit and the wings. Shards of shattered metal and glass wheeled through the air, and cloth, and flesh. One shredded wing started on fire.

Ace felt as if a monstrous hand had swatted her like a fly. Her vision wavered and her ears rang. She struggled with numb fingers to gain control of the airplane amid a sudden hurricane in the shattered cockpit.

The burning wing had no lift. The plane spiraled downward despite Ace's efforts. The terrain below was impossible. No flat landing place could be seen. Only craggy rock teeth and steep snowy slopes.

Shattering impact came soon, and along with it, oblivion.

Newsdealers will please receive their orders for the immediate issue. Globe reminders are help by taking the paper regularly.

VOL. XCI–NO. 149

Boston Evening Globe

BOSTON, TUESDAY EVENING, JUNE 7, 1921–FOURTEEN PAGES

Evening 1^C Edition

Closing Market Prices

PRICE ONE CENT

▲▲ EVENING EDITION—7:30 LATEST ▲▲

Aviatrix attempted round the world flight.

Cecilia "Ace" Carroway did not reach New Delhi, the end of the 5th leg of her 10 stage journey around the world in an airplane. No rumor of her fate has so far surfaced. The fifth leg contained a crossing of the Himalayan mountain range, which contains the highest peak in the world. Mt. Everest. The first leg was from G. Franklin Airport in Essex County, Massachusetts to Juneau, Alaska. The aircraft was a Lockheed Flyer equipped with extra fuel tanks. In custom aviation

Star-crossed life?

According to local historian Vern Lesser, Cecilia "Ace" Carroway led a tragic life. Only ten days ago, she attended the funeral of her father, Grant Carroway of Carroway shipping. Her mother was silent film actress Amiti Rishi, who died during a boating accident that left her father lamed when Miss Carroway was a tender three years of age. Miss Carroway herself was in the midst of obtaining an M.D when the Great War erupted in Europe. She enlisted as a pilot and earned ten kills over France. She master-minded an engineering

The last known photograph of aviatrix Ace Carroway, taken on the morning of her departure from G. Franklin airport on her attempt to circumnavigate the world by air. Portions of her modified Lockheed Flyer are visible in the background. Photograph by Mr. Gill Cartwright, freelance photographer based in

ONI involvement.

In a related story, the Globe has learned that on the morning of departure from G. Franklin airport, a bomb exploded near the runway. A previously convicted felon named Fabian Pugsley was taken into custody by Lt. Drew Lacy of the Hyannis, Cape Cod police department. Pugsley is the "bank vault bomber" who allegedly robbed several New York banks within the last six months. The Hyannis P.D. said the broader investigation was being handled by the Office of Naval Intelligence. The Hyannis P.D. would not speculate

NOTES

Ace's world is fictional, but of course I strive to capture the flavor of the early 20th century as much as possible. Surely, the sourpuss gumshoe is an icon of Americana every bit as much as the rattletrap Ford Model T that he drives.

The Lockheed Flyer, on the other hand, is pure fiction, though it was inspired by a real airplane made circa 1920 by the Loughhead Aircraft Mfg. Co. called the Model S-1. It incorporated a monocoque structural design. A successor company, Lockheed Corp., used many S-1 design ideas to make the record-breaking Vega aircraft in 1927. These aircraft were skinned with molded plywood.

Name-dropping of comic books (The Black Mask) and hotels (Copley Square) and many geographic details come from the world we know. Like Melville when he wrote *Moby Dick*, I have never had the pleasure of visiting Nantucket, though I have long been fascinated by pioneering astronomer Maria Mitchell and the history of the observatory that bears her name.

The Red Baron was real, of course, credited with 80 aerial victories in WWI. Major Sinclair and his heroic death are fiction. However, the English poet Laurence Binyon is not. He penned *For the Fallen* to commemorate English soldiers who had died overseas, the fourth stanza of which appears in the dedication to this slim volume.

Although by the end of this episode Ace herself has fallen, I can say with fair confidence that down is not the same as out. Ace will fly again.

ABOUT THE AUTHOR

Wyoming native Guy Worthey traded spurs and lassos for telescopes and computers when he decided on astrophysics for a day job. Whenever he temporarily escapes the gravitational pull of stars and galaxies, he writes fiction. He lives in Washington state with his violinist wife Diane. He likes cats and dogs and plays keyboards and bass guitar. His favorite food is called creamed eggs on toast, but once in a while he heeds the siren song of chocolate.

ACKNOWLEDGMENTS

Especial thanks to readers extraordinaire Christine, Jay, Jordan, and Sonya. Love and gratefulness to my family, especially Diane.

THE ADVENTURES OF ACE CARROWAY

Book 1

Ace Carroway and the Great War

Book 2

Ace Carroway Around the World

Book 3

Ace Carroway and the Handsome Devil

guyworthey.net

Made in the USA
Columbia, SC
02 April 2018